Connections
and Other Stories

Larry I. Samuels

Connections
and Other Stories

Dedication

This collection is gratefully dedicated to my dear wife Marguerite Anne, who is a perceptive writer, an excellent editor, a dedicated teacher, mentor and compassionate server, a loving mother, admired aunt, the uplifting refuge of our family, and empowers my involvement in community service; to my sister, Caren Ann, who provided literary consulting services; and to my children Paul Henry and Rebecca Marie who consistently sparkle in demonstrating their patience and love for my insufferable silliness.

January 28, 2019

Connections
and Other Stories

Table of Contents

Connections
and Other Stories

Introduction

It's been my experience during the current close to seventy years that I have been alive that it doesn't take a lot of effort to get things wrong, but you need to work hard at getting things right. This has shown itself to be the case for me in many venues – growing up with my extended family in Brooklyn, New York, attending various schools, moving countless times, working at myriad jobs, dating (since the seventh grade), serving in the U.S. Navy, being married, and having two children, just to mention a few conditions. Although these experiences may have been unique to me, it seems that most of us have shared in some of these things in one form or another.

You can certainly hurt the feelings of a lot of people if you don't watch what you are doing, and you can help many people if you have figured out how to do so. Sometimes it goes well and sometimes it doesn't. These efforts took their toll on me and others in my circle.

Along with my basic, focused, as well as non-directed living experiences, while exploring the realm of theoretical conjecture, and the world of empirical realities, these conditions have provided the material for me to write about.

My writing has been like that, getting things wrong and getting them right, trying to capture in writing the glaring and subtle errors of life, the great triumphs, and the wistful remembrances on the riverbanks of regret.

Writing from real experience and imagination is a challenge, and can result in spectacular pieces, as well as terrible disasters. Reading other writings is vital to improving one's literary products, and it is obvious that formal training and instruction can be extremely helpful. Although I have been reading voraciously over the years and have committed myself to the short story genre since middle school, I've only attended one formal creative writing class several years ago – a few weeks of an adult education group conducted by a competent author, a very insightful and thoroughly professional writer.

I, along with the ten or so of us in this class, were challenged to write several different pieces, and then were required to read them to the group for the critique. No holds barred here, this is what the class was all about – honesty and forgiveness. It was a strained and joyful experience.

I was able to improve my outlook on writing by being reminded, for example, that I needed to include more dialogue in my stories in order to move these pieces along.

I have not always been successful in this endeavor – not that my stories don't move, it's just that they sometimes do so at a very steady pace. Am I aware of my audience and what it is that I am trying to say? Absolutely, however, I'm also attentive to hearing myself talk on a personal level.

Outward and inward – there's the yin and yang of Eli Siegal's Aesthetic Realism philosophy for you. My stories are extremely personal, though I certainly am aware, and try really hard, to provide a general appeal, in a personal, selective way. If I'm guilty of writing to myself, well, then I'm guilty.

My writing has been affected by, and I completely understand, the statement made by Edward Hoagland, author of the short story collection, *The Courage of Turtles,* and *Walking the Dead Diamond River,* among other writings, that every ten words took him one hour to write. It is no empty claim, at least it has been that way for me as well. I have been laboring on and off with some of the stories in this collection for years.

I conveyed that sentiment of working at writing to Joyce Carol Oates, prolific author of the short story collection, *Upon the Sweeping Flood,* and the novel, *Them,* among many, many other writings, when I attended a presentation that she gave more than fifteen years ago at a local community college. I had eagerly secured a ticket to her talk, in anticipation of meeting one of my favorite authors, since commencing to read her works more than twenty-five years before this talk.

Her presentation was exceedingly delicious – she is an extremely serious and very humorous writer and performer. She utilizes multiple adjectives and adverbs, superbly describing and defining woeful and heroic characters who are demonstrating desperate and redeeming actions. Although this wealth of language may not be everyone's cup of tea, it has always fulfilled my thirst.

Standing on line to have her sign the two collections of her stories that I brought to the table, I was patient and excited, as others chatted with her. My turn – I told her that she was a sketch, and how much I had enjoyed and admired her work over the past two decades.

I said that I had a four-hundred-page personal memoir manuscript in development, for the past three years at that time.

I credited Edward Hoagland with his observation on the struggles of writing.

She smiled, mildly acknowledged my literary pursuits, thanked me for my loyalty, especially with the older collections that I was presenting, signed the books, and I left in a stable mode, although yearning for more. I only wanted to have had the time to really discuss her persona, her stories, writing in general, and my future. Maybe some other time.

The resolve, then, to complete any number of my stories, and to publish my work, although was somewhat intensified following our talk, I still had to face the task of completing, and editing these pieces. Up until this meeting with her, not as many of my stories had come to fruition as I would have liked to have seen. And, let alone creating new work.

These encounters of attending the writer's class and meeting Joyce Carol Oates led to the resolution that I made several years later to join another writers group. This endeavor was so productive that we members, including my wife, published a collection of prose and poetry – what an exciting time.

One member of the group pointed out to me that maybe I could focus and expand more on a selected element of a story instead of including so many tangents within one.

This advice was very helpful in my resolve to capture that technique and I worked hard enough to subsequently publish a collection of stories in 2014, my first project, *Pay the Price and Other Stories.*

In publishing my stories, I was also encouraged by reading several other works over the years, of John Updike's in his collection, *Pigeon Feathers and Other Stories.* Selections such as "The Blessed Man of Boston," "My Grandmother's Thimble," "Fanning Island," and, "Packed Dirt, Churchgoing, A Dying Cat, a Traded Car," for example, deftly, expertly, intertwine several topics together. Not that I am as enamored with myself as an equal to John Updike, far from it, but I am bolstered by the success of the construction, and language of his stories that is so appealing to so many readers. These are just some of my observations on writing.

As my wife, a former college English professor, and writer, has reminded me periodically, all writing is re-writing. And as so eloquently noted by the author David Madden in *Revising Fiction,* much to do with revision.

I don't mind that. I like writing and making corrections to writing, doing so for the past more than fifty-five years, both as a creative fiction writer, and for producing non-fiction pieces in standard business format.

I was fortunate to have this technical writing experience as one of the functions of my career position prior to retirement a few years ago, providing administrative services in facilities management and capital construction for almost thirty years at a large non-profit public service cultural institution. My business writing needed to be clear and concise, though there were ample opportunities to create enhanced prose. I also made time to labor at fiction writing as my time-stealing vocation while working in business.

I certainly make errors in my writing. An error in writing becomes a mistake, however, only when one neglects to correct it - much like life.

The stories in this collection include life's errors, omissions, corrections, and successes. As much toil and anguish as it was for me to write these stories, it has also provided me with a great sense of excitement, satisfaction, and peace. Anticipating that readers of these works will find activity and calm, I give these stories without reserve.

Connections
and Other Stories

Belonging

"I, Tommy Grants, promise to do my best, to do my duty to God and my country, to help other people at all times and to obey the Law of the Pack." He stated the Cub Scout Promise firmly, along with the five other Cub Scouts that he was standing with, facing the American Flag, the Pack Flag, and the Troop Flag. Now eleven years old, he was ending Cub Scouts, and beginning the transitional two-year WEBELOS ("We'll Be Loyal Scouts") program, on his way to becoming a Boy Scout. It was 1961, and they were meeting in a church basement in Philadelphia, Pennsylvania.

The Cub Master, Jason Allende, said, "Good job, boys, now the Law of the Pack."

The boys said in unison, "The Cub Scout follows the honored leader Akela, the Cub Scout helps the Pack go, the Pack helps the Cub Scout grow, the Cub Scout gives goodwill."

"Two," Jason said, signaling them to put their arms down, which they had been holding at a right angle, with two spread-open fingers pointing up. "Great, good job," Jason said.

Tommy felt good. He liked Scouts, he liked having friends that he saw regularly at the meetings, week after week. He belonged to something. It wasn't always easy to belong.

His father, a sales associate with a large tool company, periodically needed to move the family, which consisted of his mother, his older sister, and brother.

Everywhere they went, besides Scouts, Tommy would be a part of a new group of school friends, but that would usually come after an apprenticeship in the new neighborhood. He could remember these trials so well from at least when he was six years old. It had been difficult sometimes to fit in.

Outside of Scouts, in his 4th grade, and then 5th grade classes, and on the streets of Philadelphia, he could almost hold his own against the elements of peer pressure, even at this young age. Unfortunately, though, the demand by the other youths, which required him to smoke cigarettes, to steal from the corner fruit stand, and then to be accepted into the clique, took its toll. He had not escaped smoking in those early grades but would only steal if he felt completely invisible to the store owner.

Although Tommy possessed the inner strength to persevere in these trials, basically being a reserved and shy boy, and although he was self-sufficient, he was always forced to display more bravado than he really felt.

Street life was difficult. Scouting was not. In Scouting, there were no trials based on illegal activities. Fortunately, the acceptance and friendships within a Pack or Troop was almost instantaneous. Scouting is somewhat like being in a gang, though wholesome. There are rules. One of the unwritten rules is that the boys need to make new Scouts feel welcome.

This was the second Cub Scout Pack that he had joined, since moving to this neighborhood one year ago and now he would be moving on to join another.

His father didn't participate much in Scouting – he always seemed to be working. His mother had been a supporter of his Cub activities, when she could find the time from her various jobs in local retail stores. She was serving as a Den Mother, but for another den – mothers couldn't be leaders in the same group as their sons. No matter, one of his friends' mother was the Den Mother of Tommy's group. He liked being in her den.

She treated him well, and was a lot of fun to be around, along with the other Cubs.

His mother was with him tonight at the transition ceremony, and his father had even been able to represent himself for a change. Tommy's mother hadn't participated in Scouting with his brother, Rick, who had not joined Scouts – too much moving around, even in those days.

Unfortunately, the family was moving again, right now, to New York. This was going to be his last meeting here. Tommy would not be moving on to WEBELOS in this Pack, but would need to find a new Pack, in another town, with another group of boys.

He just never seemed to get used to the moving. No, more than that, he just never seemed to get settled enough in a new environment before he was forced to abandon whatever advances he had made in making friends, in belonging with them.

The Cub Master was asking the boys to join him at the tables that were set up for the dens' achievement activities for this night.

They were making musical instruments, drums, from empty, painted coffee cans, with both ends cut off, then using trimmed pieces of automobile tire inner tubes, which were tied on tightly with pieces of plastic lanyard.

He worked on finishing his drum by tying the last piece of lanyard. He would keep this drum even as an adult. This item, along with a patrol flag from one of his later Scout troops, and several uniforms and patches that his mother had kept from his childhood, were the tangible memories that he would have from those days.

He showed the completed project to his Den Mother, then to the Cub Master.

"Nice job, Tommy, looks good. This finishes up your crafts achievement," Jason said.

"I had a good time making this one," Tommy commented.

Jason said, "You know, Tommy, the next set of things that you'll be doing are the WEBELOS assignments in your new town. I'm sure you're going to do well in that. You were a good Scout here in this Pack."

"Yeah, I liked it here," Tommy said. "I'm going to miss you guys."

"We'll be missing you, my boy," Jason said. "But I know you're going to be okay. Scouting is one big family, no matter where they are, or in whatever group you're in."

"I hope so. I don't want to leave here but we have to move," Tommy said.

"Well," Jason said, "We want you to take what we taught you here, the self-reliance and good values that you got out of this and bring it to your new pack."

This kind of talk could be heady for an eleven-year-old, but Tommy was a mature youth. While not comfortable with change, he had faced it before and felt that he had this quality of self-esteem – he just had to continue to believe in himself which he mostly did.

Several days after this last meeting, the move was completed. Tommy was in a new city, in a new neighborhood and in a new school. His mother found the local Scout troop a few weeks later, and they went to their first meeting. Tommy's father was already on the road.

He started the program of WEBELOS activities immediately, which included some crafts, some science and some citizenship lessons. Tommy's next several meetings went well.

His WEBELOS leader, a young adult aged twenty, had achieved the highest rank in Scouting, that of Eagle. In a short time, Tommy became friendly with several of the other Scouts, some who lived nearby to Tommy in this neighborhood. They would walk together to the meetings on Tuesday evenings, and back again. Tommy was fitting in.

At the same time that he was acclimating himself with Scouts, he began to be courted by the fringe population in his new sixth grade class. These were the students who had already transitioned from cherubs to devils. It always seemed to be the lowest of the bottom-feeders that gravitated to pulling in the newest victim to their ilk.

From the first day in the new school, Rafe Green, reputed to be the toughest kid in this elementary school, latched on to Tommy. On that day, Rafe, along with several other sixth graders, surrounded Tommy in the schoolyard.

"Hey, man, where'd you come from?" Rafe had challenged Tommy.

Tommy had been through this before. "Me, I'm new, from Philadelphia," he answered.

"Yeah, what are you doing here?"

"My dad moved us because of his job." Tommy then tried an offense. "What do you want to know that for?" He balanced this challenging question without a threatening tone.

Rafe seemed surprised. Boys didn't usually talk back to his bullying self. "I don't know, just asking," Rafe said. Tommy's minor act of confidence had worked. The bell rang. "Let's take this up again at lunchtime," Rafe said.

"Take up what?" Tommy said in another tone of bravery. "I'm going into school, but I don't see what we're going to talk about, except maybe what we're having for lunch." Tommy was up-front with his steadiness but was feeling weak inside.

"Okay, my man, good enough. Let's go," Rafe directed Tommy, and the group, then headed for the building entrance.

After morning class and lunch, the boys gathered in the schoolyard for recess. Standing out of the sight of the teacher monitor, Rafe pulled out a pack of Camel cigarettes and offered one to Tommy.

"You know, all of us here smoke. How about you?" Rafe asked.

"Sure, I'll take one," Tommy said. He pulled a cigarette out of the pack, and Rafe held a match to it. Drawing in, Tommy inhaled and suppressed a cough. For the moment, he was in with the group.

"What street do you live on?" Rafe asked.

"I'm on East 17th"

"Okay, that's just around the corner from me. Why don't you come over to 18th near Churchill Avenue on Friday night about seven o'clock? We'll be outside near the corner," Rafe said.

"Friday? Alright, I'll tell my mom. What are we going to do?"

"We'll get some more smokes and maybe we'll play 'Johnny on a Pony.' You done that before, right?" Rafe asked him. This was a street game where one person was the "pillow" standing with his back to a wall, then the rest of the team members linked arms in a line, bending over, and the other team jumped on their backs, as close as they could to the pillow, with the linked team holding the jumping team on their backs for as long as possible with as many of the jumping team landing on their backs. Leave it to adolescent city kids to make this one up.

"Yeah, we did that in Philly. I'll meet you Friday night. What else will we do?" Tommy asked.

"Maybe we'll just see what else we'll do. Maybe we'll go over to Patty's house and meet up with Cindy, and with some of the other guys. Around here you gotta belong to the neighborhood or you're nothing, you know what I mean?" Rafe didn't mention a formal gang, and fortunately for Tommy this was not to be the case. Just the local youth residents near the school and the close-by streets.

"Yeah, I know what you mean," Tommy said.

"That's good. We'll see you Friday," Rafe said.

"Who's Patty and Cindy?"

"They go to Junior High and they hang out with us."

"Okay, I'll see you Friday."

Tommy had his pack and WEBELOS meetings on Tuesday nights, so he would be able to join the new school group on Friday. He could see that he would have to balance the wholesome Scouts with the rough world of the neighborhood.

It would just have to be this way. Even though he had stayed in Scouts in Philadelphia, he had also been a part of the rest of his neighborhood. While not a formal gang, it had been a loose-knit group of boys, and girls, just like it seemed to be here. Somehow, he had made it work, and would have to do the same in this neighborhood.

After supper, he told his mother that he was going to meet some of the guys on the next block.

"Be careful, Tommy," she said. "Don't do anything stupid."

"I'll be alright, mom. It's just some of the guys from school. I don't think we're going to do anything bad."

"Okay, I'll see you about nine, how's that?"

"Sure, mom, I'll see you later."

He left the apartment building and went around the corner. Rafe and a few of the others were sitting on the stoop, which is a small stone staircase ending in a platform leading to the entrance of an apartment building.

"Hey, my man, how you doin'?" Rafe asked.

"I'm alright, who's everyone here?"

Rafe said, "This here's Franky, you got Bill, that's Junior, there's Nathanial and you know Michael."

"Yeah, how you all doing?" Tommy asked.

"Welcome to the neighborhood," Bill said.

"Let's get some smokes and see what's going on over Anthony's house," Rafe said.

"I think he told me he was meeting up with Patty," said Bill.

"Sounds okay by me," Tommy said. He was adrift, but he would belong here, for a while.

A Cat Named Rabbit

Daniel, sixteen, and Gloria, fourteen, were brother and sister who lived on a forty-acre apple orchard in Newburgh, New York, until each left for college. Since their parents had died in a car accident, they had been moved to the farm, which was owned by the two remaining closest members of their mother's family, an older aunt and uncle, Betty and Joseph.

Before joining these relatives on the farm, they had been living with their parents in a row house in Yonkers, a moderately-sized city just south of Newburgh. They had visited their aunt and uncle many times while growing up, to help pick apples in the fall with other migrant workers. The apples were sold to a major supermarket in the city. It was a treat for the children, as city-dwellers, to work on the farm, with both taking turns at times driving the tractor that was connected to a tank truck for spraying the trees with insecticide or using it for plowing one of the vacant fields to plant, and then to harvest, a crop of green beans.

Although while they were living in the city, they did like being on the farm, at least to visit, it was different now, living there. In their previous life, they had walked to their schools in the neighborhood, and then had walked home again with their friends along the city streets.

Here in this small farming community they were picked up and dropped off by a school bus at the end of the farm lane. Although they had made new friends fairly quickly, they had to wear the shield of newness, and the tag of big city-folks. They felt like orphans for those first few months following the loss of their parents.

Before moving, while living in the city, they owned a pet cat named Rosie. They would let her out to forage in the narrow strip of their backyard, and then she would explore farther in the neighborhood. She would always return in the evening.

When they moved, they took her with them, and immediately let her roam outside. For several days after their arrival she would come back, like she did in the city. Soon after that, however, Rosie did not return, for several days. The children were upset. They had lost their parents, which was completely devastating, and now they had lost their dear pet.

They thought that Rosie was gone for good until one morning soon after she had disappeared, when the children were having breakfast in the kitchen. They heard a commotion outside. Each jumped up from the table, opened the door, and ran outside, followed by their aunt. There was Rosie, rummaging in the trash can, raiding the garbage, with several of the other farm cats digging in as well.

Daniel and Gloria were proud of her. They could see that apparently, she had also made friends, and was now leading the country cats, behaving like the tough city cat that she was.

Aunt Betty walked to the can, with the cats scattering themselves in all directions, and placed the cover on it. Why it had been off in the first place was not clear, but it provided a shining moment for Rosie.

If the trash cover had not been off that day, they might not have seen Rosie foraging as leader of the pack. Once the cats were gone after that raid, Daniel and Gloria didn't know if Rosie would return to the house. Unfortunately, it was to be the last time that they saw her. For whatever reason or circumstance, she never came back.

There were, however, cats that did come back to the area to see if they could scrounge more food.

The trash can, which was moved to the end of the road by their uncle on dump days for pick-up, was otherwise kept in an area near the side entrance of the house. Here is where the original well had been dug, and a hand pump installed, more than fifty years ago. The pump was no longer used for house water, since the place had been refitted for indoor plumbing some time ago, but it was fun to pump that handle, and to drink the cold fresh water that came spurting out after some vigorous pumping.

The cats that came back, hoping for the trash can lid to be off, didn't like it when the children went out there to pump the water, and would run away down the slight hill from the wellhead.

Most of them waited patiently until the children were finished squirting, to continue their stealthy approach to see if the lid was off.

Not too long afterward when Rosie left, Daniel and Gloria noticed another one of the group of cats wandering near the house. This one, a female, would come around whenever their aunt, uncle, or the children would put out an opened can of tuna, or some left-over chicken parts, or any other vittles that came from their table, in order to be nice to the cats.

The family could see that this cat seemed to be able to fend for herself for food around the farm.

There were plenty of field mice, and moles that she seemed to find, as she sometimes carried these prizes to the door of the house to show anyone who was around.

This cat was a calico, and although light-colored, kept herself very clean, despite living on the bare brown earth of the farm. As Daniel and Gloria could see that she seemed to hop-walk more than stealth-walk, maybe from some previous injury, they couldn't help but name her Rabbit. What a great name for a cat they thought.

For a while, Rabbit didn't come too close to anyone. She waited until the leftover tidbits were placed on the ground, walked away from, and then she would creep towards it to eat.

Other cats came around as well, but they didn't scrabble much for the little that was available — after all, there were other things to eat around the place.

Then the weather changed, and it became colder, and darker earlier. Rabbit changed too — she started coming closer and staying longer. The first day that it snowed she came right up to the door of the house and meowed.

Gloria opened the door and Rabbit carefully placed her head inside. That's as far as she got.

When Aunt Betty moved across the kitchen toward Rabbit, the cat bolted back out and ran behind the house. Everyone would have to wait to see if she would try it again.

Several days went by and she was still a no-show. Then there was a heavy snowfall. Daniel happened to hear her meowing by the door and opened it slowly. This time she not only placed her head inside but came fully within the kitchen.

No one moved. Uncle Joseph and Aunt Betty stayed put, Gloria was sitting at the table, and Daniel was standing at the door. Apparently sensing welcome, Rabbit took a short two hops landing under the table. Gloria reached down slowly, and tentatively scratched her neck. They heard her purr. She had found a welcoming place.

Gloria took a can of tuna from the closet and opened it, placing it on the floor under the table. Rabbit sniffed it, then started eating her banquet.

Daniel took a clean, empty container from the dishrack, filled it with water, and placed that near the tuna can. Rabbit didn't miss a bite.

After a few minutes she stopped eating, sniffed the water, and lapped up a good long drink.

Then she backed away from under the table, turned to the door and sat down on her haunches, favoring one leg.

Gloria opened the door and Rabbit hopped outside.

She would begin showing up more and more often throughout that winter, meowing at the door, and one of the family opened it for her to come inside. By this time, they had purchased a bag of cat food and a feeding bowl which they kept for these visits. Many times, Rabbit would stay in the kitchen, and was very receptive to being petted and scratched by anyone of the family, then staying through the night. The children had also placed a litter box in a corner of the kitchen for Rabbit's use. It certainly did seem that she must have lived in a domestic residence before acclimating herself to the farm life, as she seemed spayed, and now was a part of this personal scene.

Daniel and Gloria continued attending high school, with Daniel graduating, and then moving on to a local community college. Gloria completed high school and attended a college not too far away. Aunt Betty and Uncle Joseph continued to care for Rabbit as she came around, and left, and came around.

Losing their parents, and then losing Rosie, had closed one chapter in their lives. Having Rabbit come into their house was the start of a new phase.

This had helped all of them become more comfortable, as time had gone on.

They had all found a home.

Choices

The concert tickets were safely tucked into the top pocket of Cliff's worn-out pale-blue chambray shirt. The flap was buttoned over. All he had to do was hold on to them until next Saturday night, and he and his sister Miranda would be three rows back in the orchestra, center stage, listening to Neil Young performing live at Carnegie Hall.

Cliff had worked hard to secure these tickets. They had cost him $20.00 dollars each. He and Miranda were really looking forward to being there. They had followed Neil's music since way before he joined with David Crosby, Stephen Stills and Graham Nash in 1970 to record the iconic album, *Déjà Vu,* the second album that they had recorded together, as eagerly awaited as any Beatles album.

Cliff and Miranda were college students attending different schools and were just one year apart in their degree programs. Cliff was twenty-two years old and Miranda was twenty. As brother and sister, they were great friends, and would many times share in various cultural activities, along with several of their mutual friends.

Now on campus this afternoon, Cliff couldn't wait to show the tickets to Miranda.

He would see her later at home, and they would talk about when they would leave their house by subway to get to the concert, and what they thought Neil would sing.

There wasn't going to be anything that would stop them from attending this concert, he thought.

Until Janet walked up to him in one of the corridors on their way to a late class. She was only an acquaintance of Miranda's. Cliff and Janet had dated once or twice and might do so again soon. As they walked toward class, Cliff asked, "Hey Janet, how are you doing?"

"Hi, Cliff, what's going on?"

"I'm good. Guess what I have?"

"I don't know, what?"

"Right here in my pocket are two tickets to see Neil Young at Carnegie Hall."

"You're kidding? How did you get them? They are really scarce."

"You know it. I traveled all the way to a ticket outlet in Queens somewhere that had some left. Now I've got them, and I can't wait to go, with Miranda."

"Let me get this straight. You've got Neil Young tickets and you're going with your sister?"

"Well, yeah. It's something we figured we'd do. You know we do things together, me and her."

"Yeah, I know you mentioned your sister a couple of times when we went out, but I didn't know it was serious."

"Janet, it's not serious — we grew up together and we're good friends."

"Well, I'm your friend, too, and you know what? I really, really love Neil Young. Let me ask you this — what would it take for you to share those tickets?"

They had stopped walking for a moment and she was looking at him full in his face.

"How about if I offer something to you that you just can't live without? Why don't I invite you over to my house this Friday night? My folks won't be home and we can have a special evening that you will be very, very happy about, and then we can go to the concert together the next week."

Cliff stood very still, but he reached up with one hand to touch his pocket. Janet was standing just as still, but she reached up with one hand to touch Cliff's shoulder.

An enticing offer thought Cliff, for one long moment. He also thought that Janet was a very desirable creature. Then he thought about Miranda. While spending an evening with Janet was extremely tempting, his sister Miranda was important. He could not betray her for one evening of pleasure.

"Janet, what a nice suggestion, and I sure would enjoy spending the night with you, but I have to tell you that I need to skip it in respect to Miranda. Sorry we can't go to the concert together, but that's just the way it has to be."

"Too bad, Cliff, you could have had a spectacular time at my house, and we could have had a great time at the show, but you know, I get it, and I can't complain."

"That's good. Glad we're on the same page here."

"We may be on the same page," Janet said, "but just remember what you gave up."

"I'll keep that in mind," Cliff said, "But I know Miranda won't be disappointed, and maybe you and I will take this up again sometime."

"We'll see, Cliff, we'll see. Give me some time to recover."

"Sure, let me see if I can get some tickets to someone else who you'd like to hear live. Maybe that would work," he said.

"It would have to be as good as Neil, but you give it a good try and let me know."

They continued to class walking together, not saying another word.

The Proposal

It was hard that cold, dry day for Frank and Melody. They were sitting on a couch in a friend's apartment, each looking away from the other.

"You know," Frank said turning back to her, "I'm as uncomfortable as you seem to be."

"Really?" she said. "I don't picture you ever being uncomfortable about anything. You are the most confident person I have ever known. I'm here with you now and talking to you about myself because if I wasn't talking to you, I would be talking to a Priest."

"Wow," he said. "That makes me feel even more uncomfortable. I kind of think of myself as a good listener, but I hadn't thought of myself in those lofty terms. I'm here for you, Melody. I'm glad you feel that way."

"If it wasn't so strange to be in this apartment in the middle of the day, I think I could relax," she said.

"You can relax with me, Melody. By what you just said you seem to be able to trust me."

"That's just the trouble," she said, "I trust you — it's me that I can't trust."

Frank stared at her for a moment. He hadn't thought of her being in that kind of conflict at all. He only thought of her struggling with her giving him permission to proceed.

It was usually he who would be doing the pursuing, and it was he who wanted to go further than just talking, to engage in some intense petting, or more than that. Here was someone who was thinking the same thing.

"Well," he said, "you know we could do some other things. It doesn't have to be that we go all the way."

"I know," she said. "I'm not worried about you. You wouldn't dream of taking advantage of me. It's me that I'm worried about."

As Frank started to process this revelation, he thought back to a time during middle school when he had attended a birthday party with some classmates for one of the girls. Following cake and presents, with her parents upstairs, and the guests in the basement, the afternoon's festivities had led to a game of "Spin the Bottle, Seven Minutes in Heaven." Here was a variation worthy of middle school students. Not only did two students get to kiss quickly in front of everyone, but then they were able to disappear into another room to take care of whatever it was they were going to do, for seven minutes.

Frank had no illusions that he was going to get anywhere important with one of the other guests, Kathie, who had spun the bottle that was pointing at him. She was a fairly shy girl, though friendly, and was well-liked by the others.

While he thought about that day, he remembered that he had hardly ever spoken to Kathie, let alone had ever been anywhere with her, even in a crowded room, or in a class.

They had kind of embraced and kissed each other, then they stood up from the circle, and walked to the next room, with the other students giggling and calling to them to be careful in there.

Once in the room, with the lights out, standing up, she had come right over to him, circled her arms around his neck and pulled his face to hers. This was more than an illusion. She had given him a long, intimate kiss, holding him tightly. Shocked for one moment, he had kissed her back, and had placed his arms around her waist. In the midst of this kiss, he had started to grope further down from her waist and pressed himself more tightly to her. She had moved her hands down his back and had pulled him closer too. He had remembered the next six minutes being busy with searching, stroking, feeling, and groping.

That's as far as they had gone. After all, they were still at a public party.

Finally, someone had knocked on the door. "Time's up, you two," a voice had sung out.

Frank and Kathie had straightened their clothes and had spilled out of the room. The crowd had just looked at them — whatever comments they might have wanted to say, no one had said anything.

Then one of the other girls had said, "Okay, who's next?" The game had resumed, but Frank and Kathie were done. For whatever reason, certainly one of them being their youth, Frank and Kathie had never pursued their tentative exploring during the rest of the school year. It had been just a dreamy, tentative moment.

Remembering that time in middle school, now still thinking about Melody's comment, Frank didn't say anything in response to her disclosing that she was unsure of holding herself in check.

Frank was young, a junior in college. Melody was even younger, a sophomore. Here they were together on this stark afternoon, each not having classes this day. Frank knew that she wasn't very experienced sexually, as she had told him that. Even he wasn't all that experienced either. But he had ideas, and apparently, so did Melody.

What had brought them together in this setting was an experiment in being alone together in a private place, in the apartment of another student, a mutual friend.

Frank and Melody had been dating for a few months after meeting through a friend of Melody's. Once they started seeing each other regularly, it was just inevitable, for them, anyway, that they would be drawn to becoming closer, physically.

Frank was basically a shy, gentle person. He used his large size, though, as a buffer between his gentle ways and his determination to succeed. He too, although presenting an imposing appearance, was really kind, and a good listener.

Melody, while not overly demonstrative in her emotions, was nonetheless a little more outgoing than Frank. Her demeanor always put Frank just on the leading edge of expectancy, though he stayed calm.

Melody put herself in front of people like she just stepped out of a fashion magazine ad, but one found out immediately that she was not pretentious, or haughty, or anything other than friendly and kind.

Their being here in this space in this situation seemed strange to them as they spoke, and they were uncomfortable, but they were only uncomfortable with themselves being there.

They were not wholly uncomfortable with each other.

"Melody," Frank began, "I'm not sure that we can spend the next couple of hours sitting here talking about what we're going to do or not going to do. I don't know if I can take this uncertainty. I would just as soon call it a day and go out to a movie or something."

She didn't say anything, nor did she look up. Then, "Frank, I know you're right, but I'm not ready to give up yet. Don't you still want to see if you can get into my pants?"

Frank gulped. "Uh, Melody, I thought you just said that if you weren't here talking with me now, you'd be confessing to a Priest."

"That's what I said, but not exactly what I meant. What I tried to make you understand is that I am really ready to move ahead sexually with you, but I'm so torn between being casual about it, and it being meaningful."

"Honey, there's nothing casual about this at all. I've been up front with you since we started to get to know each other. I'm still a virgin, but with some skin contact, and so are you, and yes, we're both kind of new at this. I wouldn't want anything to come between our liking each other for who we are right now, and I'm getting the feeling that you want it that way too."

"I get it now," he continued, "since I heard you say it, that you're not so sure that you want it to get physical, but you really want it to be physical. This conversation is getting a little out of hand for me, so to not spoil anything, I'm going to stop talking."

They sat there for a minute. Melody looked up. "Frank, you are saying it right, and I really have to decide."

"No, Melody, you don't have to decide anything today. Just that you're still unsure is enough for me. I don't want to keep wrestling with this. I'm going to make this next decision, and I'm going to stick to it, even though I'm cutting off what I'm sure will be some really great sex today. Here's my proposal – you and I should just pack up, walk out the door, and go back to my car, holding hands. For the next few months of this semester, why don't we just keep going out, keep working on homework together when we can help each other, and we'll see some time later if we still can't keep our hands off each other, then maybe we'll see if this apartment, or some other place, is available. What do you think about that?"

"You know," she said, "I didn't have to talk to a Priest, I've got you."

"Yeah, well, I can be my own worst enemy."

"You may be your own worst enemy, Frank, but you're my best friend."

Shipping Out

Was there ever a time when it had been easy in those days of wartime to decide the best course? Allen Hodges didn't think so. He was torn, now nineteen years old, and one year out of high school — stay where he was taking classes at the local community college, or seek a path through some branch of the military, other than the Army? In 1969, it was impossible to avoid being caught up in the war raging in Vietnam.

And he was involved in a relationship.

Maria Alvarez was exotic, an imp of the Barrio. She was thin, and dark, with black hair, street-smart, a student at the college, and fun. Allen was slight, had blond hair, was a marginal student, and serious. He and Maria were in a required beginning Italian language class together that first year and had struck up a conversation one day early in the semester while sitting next to each other.

"So, what brings you to college?" Allen had asked her.

"I need to find a career out of my neighborhood," she had answered.

"Yeah, sounds like a great idea. What are you thinking of?"

"Well, maybe psychology, or sociology, not too sure yet. I just know I need to move ahead."

"I know what you mean," Allen had said. "But I really don't know what I'm going for. I just know that I'm staying out of the Army for the time being, until my money runs out."

"Oh, that," she had said. "I don't know how many guys are here in school doing just that, but I can guess."

"It's a mess alright," he had said. "There are very bad things going on over there, horrible things, and no one, well, most no one, knows what it's for."

"Well, I don't have to deal with that," she had said. "I'm a woman, and don't have to bother with any of that, but I know it must be terrible for you. Most of the guys in my neighborhood get out of high school and go right into the Army. It's been like this for the past few years. We had a couple of the boys, from just a few blocks away, who didn't make it back." She had looked off to a corner of the room when she had described this lament.

"I'm really sorry, for them, and their families," Allen had said. "Some of the guys from my high school graduated, then were drafted. I know of one guy who didn't make it back either. I had heard about it from someone I know who knew his brother."

She went on. "I have an older brother who's twenty-eight and he's out of it. He works at a hospital in maintenance in Local 1199 and got an exemption for doing an essential job."

"That's a pretty good gig for him," Allen had said. "I guess lots of guys would want to find something that gets them out of the draft, instead of going to Canada or something, or to just get it over with, and go into the Army. Maybe you need to go into the Army to be an American, but maybe you don't need to be killed to prove it. And staying in school for a deferment is probably one of the most elitist privileges of the white middle class that anyone invented, but it works for me."

"Oh, you do see that, right? Well, I'm from Puerto Rico," she had said, "but about as American as you can get, and I have no clue about what we're doing in Vietnam."

"Really, where in Puerto Rico?"

"From San Juan itself," she had answered. "Now here in Brooklyn at eighteen, since I was seven years old."

"Where in Brooklyn are you?" he had asked.

"Red Hook. How about you?"

"I'm over in East Flatbush. And my family is from Ireland back in the day, but my parents and I were born here."

"I've been in Flatbush, to go to the movies, and I went ice skating in Prospect Park a couple of times with the crew," she had said.

"Well, I've been to Red Hook a couple of times to visit a friend of mine on West Ninth Street just off Columbia."

"Wow, I live across from Coffey Park on Verona Street near Dwight. It is tough to get around by subway, that's for sure. Only the "F" train goes over to Smith-Ninth Street, then it's a hike to get to where you want to go, or a bus."

"I tell you what, though," he had said, "I have a car, and maybe I could pick you up and we could go out. We could get some Italian homework done, if you like."

"Well, I don't know about the Italian homework help, since I'm doing okay because I speak Spanish, but going out would be fine. *¿A dónde me vas a llevar?*"

"Oh, I got '*a donde*,' like where, right?"

"You did get part of it, *sí*. Where you going to take me?"

"Well, we could see a movie, or something."

"Sure, or something," she had responded.

"Alright, let me have your address."

He had written her address in his notebook. "And how about this Friday night?" he had asked.

"Friday works for me. But let me tell you this. Instead of you coming up to my house, I'm going to meet you downstairs in front of the building. I live with my mother, and my brother, and let's see how this date works out before you meet *mi familia*. That's the way we should do this."

"Okay, sure. I'll wait for you out front."

They settled on a time, and that's how it had started.

It was Friday. He had driven over through Windsor Terrace, Park Slope, under the six-lane elevated Brooklyn-Queens Expressway, and into her neighborhood, about eight miles from the apartment house that he lived in with his parents, and two sisters. He had found a place to stop his car, a worn-out 1961 Chevy Impala, in front of her building.

In a moment she was there, and in his car.

"Nice to see you, Maria. You look great."

"Thanks. Nice car, Allen. It's great to have a ride in the city."

"Yeah, I worked all through high school at a grocery store to get the scratch together to get this heap. Beats walking."

"One of these days I'll get one myself," she had said.

They had pulled away from the curb, turning on the next block to head to a movie theatre not too far away on Fifth Avenue near Union Street.

This was the first of several dates to other movies, to go bowling, to the rides and food at Coney Island, and to join with other friends, both Maria's and Allen's, meeting in front of her house, or at other locations. Allen had wondered about not meeting her mother and brother, but he didn't question it. To him, Maria was mature, independent, and capable of handling herself. She must know what's best, he had thought

He had brought her to his house one evening after they had gone out a few times, and she had met his mother and father, and his sisters, who were still in high school, though two grades apart. His family didn't blink that he was dating a Puerto Rican woman. To them, she was just a nice, friendly person.

They had moved forward through the next two months, attending class, until Allen had suggested that they could have a stay-at-home night at the apartment of one of his cousin's.

His cousin and his wife would not be home until late that evening and had offered Allen and Maria this time for them to be there.

Maria had been fine with this. That evening, they had eaten at a local diner, then had bought some wine, and had spent a satisfying evening in the apartment.

Three more months had gone by. They had managed to continue dating, to socialize with friends, and had promoted another location where they could be alone from time to time. A friend of theirs from school, who was attending part-time, was working various night shifts as a supermarket manager, and had graciously provided them with the opportunities to relax at his apartment.

Their commitment to each other was growing stronger. They had even discussed their plans for the summer following the semester break and had hinted at other long-term goals. It was dreamy, and exciting.

As long as Allen remained enrolled in school, even while working a few days a week as a baker's helper in a retail shop not too far from Maria's neighborhood, he was safe from the draft.

Maria had secured a job in a variety store in between her classes. Everything was fine so far.

Then one evening Maria had invited Allen to meet her family before they were to go out. She had not provided any warning for what he was about to walk into.

He had parked on her block, had entered her building, and had climbed the stairs to the second floor. He rang her bell.

"Hey, Allen, how you doing? Please come in."

He stepped into a small foyer, then she led him into the living room. Her mother was sitting on the couch.

"Mama, this is Allen from my class. Allen, my mother, Mrs. Alvarez."

"*¿Buenos noches, Senora, como esta usted?*" he had said pleasantly.

Maria had smiled at him. "How nice," she had said.

Her mother had answered, "*Muy Bueno, mi nino, gracias.* And, how are you? You speak Spanish?"

"*Muy poquito, muy malo.*"

"That's okay," she had said, "very nice to try. Please sit down."

Before he took the next step towards a chair, Maria's brother Jose, a stocky, unsmiling, impressive-looking figure, had walked into the room.

Allen had stuck out his hand anyway, and said, "*¿Que pasa, mi amigo?*"

"Don't give me that '*que pasa*' stuff my man, I don't know you, and I don't need to know you, I just need to know that you, white boy, won't be messing with my sister anymore."

Now Maria had not set the stage here for Jose's animosity. Not a word. And she hadn't responded to this exchange. Nor did her mother. Allen was not a wallflower. He was prepared to take Maria to the movies, and to other places. Taking a bold step, he said, "I'm sorry you feel that way. I don't mean any harm, it's just that Maria and I are just getting to see if we can be friends."

"Friends? What do you mean by that? Maria has friends, and they are all Puerto Ricans. She don't mess with no white guys."

Allen had stood silently. Maria finally broke in. "Jose, *mi hermano, por favor,* stay out of my business. You don't know anything about Allen. I don't even know everything about him, but we do like each other, and he seems okay."

"I don't care anything about what you think," Jose had said. "I'm telling you, buddy, there's nothing here that you need to come back for. Just you remember that good."

Then he had turned around and walked out of the room.

Mrs. Alvarez just stared at Jose's disappearing frame. Maria looked at her mother, then at Allen.

"Mama, we need to go," she had said.

"Nice to meet you, Mrs. Alvarez. Hope to see you again."

"I don't think that will work," her mother had said without tone. "Jose runs our house."

"That is too bad," Allen had said.

"Let's go," Maria had said.

They sat in his car for a while.

"No wonder you didn't want me to meet the family. Your mom seems nice, but your brother, what's his deal?"

"He's seen *West Side Story* too many times. That bit about Maria, Tony, the Sharks, and the Jets really got to him."

"I'm guessing he must have seen the latest *Romeo and Juliet* movie too," Allen had said.

"Yeah, he's got drama alright. But his intentions are good."

"Intentions? To keep you apart from anyone except another Puerto Rican guy, and from me? I'm all on your side, honey."

"I know."

Their discussion for the rest of that night had not been pleasant. It was a sad, and angry evening. If only they could live together somewhere, or could get married, that is where the conversation had gone. But it was not to be.

Reconciling with her brother did not seem to be an option. With their educational plans, and possibly the Army in Allen's future, where could they take this, now?

As hard as this was, they had concluded that they could not go on from this point.

"Maria, this is really bad. I want to be with you so much. I'm seeing us together for a long time to come."

"Allen, this can't happen. I will never get my brother to understand about people like us. We're young, and there's not so much time behind you and me yet, and too much time ahead of us, to wait until we can be free of this. If you stay stuck in school, you can be around, but it won't solve us being together. If you don't stay, you may be gone to the war. This is no way for us to live."

"You're right," he had said. "We might as well call it over, tonight."

After that episode, Maria had continued in school, and had registered for the next semester.

Allen had not enrolled for the next term, but had continued working at the bakery, filling in by pumping gas at a station near the Gowanus Expressway, on the edge of Red Hook.

And the 1A draft classification had arrived soon after, but before he had received his draft notice. That was all he needed – soon after the notice he had then enlisted in the U.S. Navy.

Disappearing into the military on the oceans of the world would remove him from ground operations in Vietnam, but it would not remove Maria from his heart.

Religious Instruction

When Dennis was in his middle school-years he turned for support to the most encompassing element that influenced his life at the time – the small group of students who were independently proceeding towards sustenance by crime.

It started with breaking open cigarette machines, not an easy task, for small change. It progressed to their big score by breaking into the back door of a general merchandise store that was not alarmed, pilfering small items that they could carry in shopping bags, like radios and toasters which they sold to willing purchasers in the neighborhood. It really didn't amount to much, didn't last very long, and they were never caught before they just stopped their crime spree. Thank goodness, no felony record to drag around.

When he turned eighteen years old in 1965 and had been graduated from high school with the completion of several shop courses in auto mechanics, he went to work at a local service station and garage.

He performed routine mechanical procedures, from changing tires, to completing basic tune-ups, to pumping gas, while still living at home with his parents, two brothers, and two sisters.

After three years on the job, he had progressed to more complicated repairs, like full engine rebuilds, but he was losing interest, was not making enough money and had tired of living with lots of family and the limited opportunities of having a clearly defined career path. Rather than wait what seemed to be the inevitable drafting into the Army, he left home to enlist in the United States Navy.

The war in Vietnam was fully engulfing the nation, and he was prepared to be involved, but first he needed training at Boot Camp in Great Lakes, Illinois, for thirteen weeks. This included instruction in military regulations, shipboard routines, firefighting, physical fitness exercises, and even adopting religion.

It was a requirement in those days that each recruit must attend a church service every Sunday morning during the time that they were in camp. As Dennis' family had only attended the local Congregational protestant church services basically on Christmas, Good Friday and Easter while he was growing up, he did not have a particular preference for attendance during Boot Camp.

His camp religious experience then started first with attendance at the Methodist service, then the Lutheran, followed by Roman Catholic, then Baptist.

Before he could decide which one he was going to attend next, one of his buddy's, Harold, the boot company clerk, a Chinese American Catholic from Pennsylvania who was also exploring, said to him, "Guess what? I found out that if we go to the Jewish services on Friday nights, then we don't have to get up on Sunday mornings to go to church."

"Really?" Dennis said. "Sounds like a good deal. I'm with you; let's do it."

That next Friday evening after chow, in full dress blue uniforms, they walked from their barracks across the training camp and through a gate onto the adjacent main Navy base.

There were several churches on the base as well as a Jewish temple. Dennis and Harold were greeted warmly by the Rabbi, and by several of the worshippers, which even included females — wives and daughters of worshiping members, consisting of Commissioned Officers and other Petty Officers serving on the base. These women were decidedly off-limits to Dennis and Harold, but they could look.

Not that it mattered much either way to Dennis or Harold who was in attendance or what the service would consist of. They were not opposed to religious instruction, but they were essentially there to fulfill their military obligation.

Following a friendly, spiritual service, though different than the Christian format, they were invited to share in something called an Oneg. This is an informal gathering on a Friday evening to celebrate the Sabbath and the joy to be found in it.

It is a social function with conversation, small sandwiches, other snacks, and it was certainly as much a coffee hour as Christians might participate in after a church service.

Members of the congregation were interested in Dennis and Harold's attraction in attending this Friday evening service and they were able to present a polite and believable affirmation of their seeking an enhanced experience.

Afterward, walking back to camp before Taps at 2200 hours, that is, at 10:00 p.m., Harold said, "So, what do you think?"

"This works for me," Dennis said. "I would come back. This seems like a great plan. We're sleeping in on Sunday."

"You got that right," Harold said.

"What about the religious part?" Dennis asked.

"You mean for me? I don't know. Like I told you, I was raised a Catholic, but I haven't been practicing much for a long time. Being in all of this prep training for war kind of makes me turned-off on the God thing too. What about you?"

"Well, like I was telling you," Dennis said, "I wasn't raised with much religion, and until boot camp I wasn't thinking of picking it up again. I'll go to the Jewish services again, so that I don't have to get up early on Sundays while we're here in camp. Otherwise, it don't make me no never mind."

"I'm with you then buds," Harold said. "Fridays it is until we're out of here."

The remaining several weeks were uneventful. They went to their shipboard training classes, continued physical exercise, endlessly practiced the sixteen-point count manual of arms with their 1903 Springfield pieces for their graduation ceremony, and attended Jewish services.

Another special highlight of the Friday night excursions following services on the main base that they discovered placed them in the path of the Enlisted Men's Club.

This bar, restaurant, and recreation building was just so convenient for them to stop in for a quick beer before heading back to the barracks.

Although they described their adventures to several other recruits when they returned in the evening, they never did generate enough interest among the group for anyone to forsake church to join them. This was fine with Dennis and Harold, keeping this niche to themselves.

Then camp was over.

Dennis, Harold, and the other eighty men in the company left for various places around the globe. Some of the men went on to specialized training schools before joining the fleet where others went directly to their duty stations. Harold, in the Naval Reserve, went back to Pennsylvania and would attend monthly reserve meetings with a two-week stint each year in the fleet.

Dennis went on to receiving a few weeks of supplemental training in shipboard mechanical engineering and was then assigned to a destroyer serving in the Gulf of Tonkin.

The ship was providing gunfire support for ground operations in Vietnam and was performing other combat related functions in coordination with aircraft carriers.

Based on his auto mechanics job skills, his rating was designated as a Machinist Mate, working and standing watches in one of the engine rooms on this destroyer, operating various pumps, monitoring the salt water evaporators, the electrical generators and regulating the steam throttle valve powering one of the turbines to drive the ship through its maneuvers and missions.

While it seemed to Dennis that he did not need to rely on any strengths or reassurances that religion could have provided while now serving in the war, he held the comfort of a peaceful time at camp having participated while there in what was almost religious instruction.

Snow Tires

The weather hadn't changed yet. It was still cool, but not cold, even though it was November. William had driven up to New York City from Charleston, South Carolina just five months earlier, where it had been hot and humid.

He was just separated from four years of active duty in the U.S. Navy. While he would still need to wait two more years following his inactive reserve obligation before receiving his Honorable Discharge, that day, he had exchanged farewells with his shipmates, had left the ship, and had walked to his car at the end of the pier on the Charleston Navy base. He had packed the car the night before with his sea bag, and now he had headed home one-thousand miles to New York City.

His intent had been to buy snow tires in Charleston, before heading North, just to be prepared for bad weather, but the shops in the area only had for sale what they called mud tires. Figures, he thought. They didn't call this section of South Carolina the low country for nothing — it sure was moist.

It was late in 1973, and all-weather tires were not readily available yet throughout the country. In the northern climates, almost everyone changed from their regular tires to snow tires, with deep, specially-cut treads, mounting them on the rear wheels, for rear-wheel drive cars, which most were then. It was what people did in those days.

William had been planning on going home for quite some time. His service days as an electrician Petty Officer, while generally a positive experience, had also been filled with relentless work, and sustained stress while his ship had operated in the Gulf of Tonkin under fire during the war in Vietnam, which was still going on. He had rotated back to the United States after two years in the Gulf, being next attached to a ship homeported in Charleston, and had traveled on board to several other parts of the world. It was his time now to be a civilian again.

He had purchased his car, a pristine 1965 Ford Mustang, from one of the used car-lots near the base a few months before his separation. He was looking forward to the drive North, and yes, even to the task of switching to snow tires.

Once he was in New York, and had visited his family, he rented an apartment not far from his old neighborhood where he had lived before enlisting.

While these first few months following active duty were occupied with part-time work renovating residential properties for a cousin-in-law of his who owned a construction firm, he wasn't thinking much about his future beyond that. He was mostly concentrating on his new-found freedom, focusing on coming and going as he pleased, and meeting women.

He looked up some old flames from the days before he had enlisted, and had a fleeting date or two, but they did not move forward.

And it happened one evening, as he was transporting the removed regular tires through the street from his car, since installing the newly-purchased snow tires (again, that's what people did), that he met one of his neighbors.

A woman who seemed to be approximately his age, in her mid-twenties, and wearing dark slacks and a stylish jacket, entered the building behind him. As he rolled the tire toward the elevator, she asked, "What's that you have there?"

William looked at her. "I'm in the middle of changing out snow tires," he answered.

"I kind of figured," she said, "but why bring this one into the building?" The elevator stopped, and they stepped in. William pressed the third-floor button.

"Well," he said, I don't really have any other place to put my regular tires, but one of the closets in my apartment was just made for them."

"I guess you don't have much else in there," she said.

"Not really. I have a bunch of things on shelves so there's plenty of room on the floor. As a matter of fact, I need to go back to the car to get the other tire. I'll store them here until after the winter."

"I don't have that storage problem," she said. "My brother and sister-in-law have a garage at their house, and I keep my tires there."

"That's handy," William said. By this time, the elevator stopped at his floor. She had pressed the fourth-floor button.

"Before we go on with this conversation, what might be your name?" he asked.

"I'm Beverly."

"Well Beverly, I'm William, and maybe if you're not busy right now we could continue this discussion after I take in the other tire. I could ring your bell when I'm done and washed up, maybe for coffee. What apartment are you in?"

She smiled. "Okay, we can do that. I'm in 402."

"Great, give me a few minutes and I'll ring for you. I'm in 307 by the way."

"Sure, see you in a little while," she said.

"I won't be more than about a half-hour," he said.

This seemed really pleasant, thought William. He stepped out of the elevator, rolled the tire through the hall, unlocked his door, and placed the tire in the closet. He went back down to retrieve the other one from the car trunk, took care of that, cleaned up, and went to the fourth floor.

They greeted each other again, and Beverly invited him to the kitchen table. Like William's three-room apartment, Beverly's was similar, with a kitchen, living-room, and one bedroom.

"So," he began, "Are you changing your own tires?"

"No," Beverly said, "I can change a flat if I have to, but I just bring my car over to my brother, and he changes them out."

"No matter what, we are consumed with snow tires, that's for sure," he said.

"It's our twice-yearly pilgrimage alright," she said.

"What are you driving?" he asked.

"I have a '67 Chevy Camaro, which I really like."

"Yeah, great car. Hot. I'm driving a '65 Mustang."

"That's pretty nice too," she said.

"What kind of work do you do?" he asked.

"Well, I've been with the City Finance Department for a few years in their tax assessment records section. What do you do, William?"

"Me? I'm just out of the Navy a few months ago as an electrician, but right now, I'm doing some general construction work until I get wise to myself. Do you like what you're doing for the City?"

"It's okay. I graduated High School five years ago with a commercial diploma and just kind of fell into this, but it's a secure job. Don't know if I'll stay there, but it'll do for now. I'm only twenty-four, so I have a long career ahead of me for work. You were in the Navy? What was that like?"

"It was interesting, had its good parts, and its bad. We worked hard, but I saw a lot of different places. I made out alright. I was separated from active duty with having a car, an expensive camera, some stereo equipment, the GI Bill, and a trade to fall back on. Not bad. And I'm twenty-six, so I have a ways to go, too."

"You could tell me more about the travel," she said. "I'd be interested in hearing about that. Oh, coffee's ready," she announced.

"Thanks, Beverly. Sure, we could go down memory lane some evening to several different countries that I've been to. It was interesting. But what else would you want to do? Are you a bowler, a movie goer, a roller skater? Are you free for any of that?"

"I'm game for most any of those things," she said. "When would you want to start?" This certainly seemed pretty friendly of her.

"How about we go out this Friday night? We could pick a movie. I'm sure there must be one over on Flatbush Avenue, or Kings Highway around 8:00 o'clock. Is that a good time for you?"

"Sounds about right. I get home from work around six. Did you want to have something to eat first? What time do you get home from work?"

To William, this conversation was going very well. She seemed relaxed. He felt relaxed and easy.

"I'm pretty flexible. The construction crew I'm with now knocks off around four since we start work at seven in the morning. If you need a little time before stepping out for dinner, why don't you call me when you're ready and I can meet you downstairs in the lobby."

"That's a plan that works just great," she said. She stood up and took a pad and pencil from one of the counter tops.

"Let me have your number, and here's mine," as she wrote it down. "Why don't you look for a couple of movies this week, and when I call you, we can figure out what to see."

"Sounds good to me," he said.

They continued chatting about the high schools that they went to, the neighborhood they were living in, cars, working, and their families. They called it a night after about an hour, and William left, not only thinking about snow tires.

Train Wreck

In the midst of those dark days following his divorce, there was a woman who had motivated Nathan to repaint his kitchen. Her example of striking hard on a domestic endeavor involving preparing and executing the repainting of her kitchen had struck a chord with Nathan. Even though the relationship with this woman had not progressed very far, the recall of how she had influenced his own project would be a memory that he would draw on for years to come.

The apartment that he was living in since ending the marriage with his former wife had been adequate, though dreary and it seemed to inspire Nathan to move forward in seeking another meaningful relationship. Dating Tina had filled a gap in the rift of human contact that had resulted from the divorce, but it had only been a station on the route, and then he had needed to move on.

While it lasted, though, Tina and Nathan had been dating for several months since they had been introduced by a mutual friend, a co-worker of Nathan's. Nathan was working as a designer in a small commercial advertising firm and Tina was working in a restaurant. Thinking that Tina and Nathan might hit it off, the friend had invited him to meet her at lunch.

Sitting there in the restaurant that day and spinning off in talking about work and relationships with his friend, Tina approached their table, as pre-arranged.

"Hey Jesse, how you doing?" she had asked.

"I'm good, Tina, I'd like you to meet my friend, Nathan. Nathan, this is Tina."

Nathan half-stood and held out his hand. "Nice to meet you, Tina."

She shook his hand. "Yes, Jesse said he would bring you around today, so it's nice to meet you, too." Without any further pre-amble or reaction to meeting Nathan she said, "Since I'm working this table, can I get you something?" Nathan was looking at her, a slim woman about his age, mid-thirties, with short black hair and dark eyes.

Jesse spoke, "I'll have coffee and a tuna sandwich on rye toast."

Nathan said, "I'll take coffee, and a ham and Swiss on whole wheat toast."

"I'll be right back," Tina said.

"So, what do you think?" asked Jesse.

"I don't know, I just said hello and ordered lunch. Not much to tell here."

"Well, you'll ask her out, right?"

"Okay, sure, I'll try that after we eat. Maybe this wasn't the best way to do this. It is a little awkward."

"Well, maybe not, but at least you two were able to see each other before you go out."

"I don't know if that was so important," Nathan said. "But anyway, here we are."

Tina brought their food, and Nathan was able to exchange just a few more words with her, quickly about work and time constraints.

She was almost friendly, in a waitressy way, but Nathan was hopeful and engaged enough to ask her out, which she had been expecting.

That next week, on a Friday evening, Nathan approached the door of her apartment, and pressed the doorbell.

She opened the door. "Hello, Nathan. Come in," she said.

He crossed the threshold, sticking out his hand, which she took.

"Thanks. Nice to see you again, Tina," he said.

He was about two inches taller than her 5'-4" height. He was blonde with blue eyes and of medium build, to her slight figure with her dark hair and he could now see brown eyes.

Each of them in their early thirties, he was optimistic of a friendly evening without controversy, and she was expecting someone who would accept her son.

"Sit down, Nathan," she invited him, which he did where she indicated on the couch.

"I know you said that your son Billy would be with your mom tonight, so I'm guessing that's why I'm not meeting him right now."

"Yeah, honestly, I didn't want for my son to be a part of this date on the first try."

"Makes sense," he said. "I can meet him some other time."

"Well, let's cross that bridge when we come to it," she said.

Nathan stopped short. He hadn't meant to place any agenda on the evening, or its future. He had just thought he was being cheerful. He had tried to rescue the moment. "Sorry, I didn't mean to get beyond this evening. I was just being sociable."

"That's okay," she had said. "Sometimes I get the wrong impression. I've been divorced a few years and have met some frogs in that time."

"Well, I'm no prince in sheep's clothing," he had said. "But I've been divorced for a while myself and need to navigate through every new encounter, without a clear map."

"I know what you mean," she had said. "It's not easy out there, but I've been managing."

"It's been a slice for me, too, but I'm moving ahead."

"Speaking of which," she had said, "Why don't we get going to dinner."

"Yes, you're right, we should go. I figured we would take my car to this Polish restaurant over in Greenpoint. I've been there before with one of my brothers and it's a nice place."

"I cook some great Italian food," she had said, "so this could be interesting."

They drove to the restaurant, talking about their living in the city, traffic and the gritty neighborhood that they were driving through, near the waterfront. She had said that her son was in first grade at the local public school, and that her mom was available for picking him up from school and for taking care of him in the afternoons.

Once at their table and after ordering, Nathan had asked her, "So, how long have you been at your restaurant?"

"Five years," she had said, "but I've been thinking about going back to school to get my Bachelor's in accounting. I would have jumped ship a while ago, but I've been raising my son alone for the past four years since my divorce, and I really need the steady income."

"That's a grind," he had said. "I can see how hard wait staff work. Dealing with customers who might not always get it can be difficult."

"Yeah," she had said, "it's sort of okay since my ex provides child support only mostly, sometimes so I have to make it work. It's been tough chasing him down."

"That's too bad about child care," he said. "that must be a sad situation. I know that can happen a lot in relationships."

"What about you," she asked. "Have you been working at your place for a while?"

"For me, I've been working at my company about six years, after I finished my Bachelor's in Economics, but I also had some kind of a talent for art work, and through a relative of mine, I was able to get an interview for this company that advises clients on advertising campaigns and sells them artwork as well."

"That's pretty good," Tina had said, "must be interesting."

"Yeah, I've been liking it and thinking I'm staying around for the future. We're moving more and more into computer aided design and such so I've been attending some training on a new system we purchased."

"Well," she had said, "even the restaurant has gone computerized, changing out our standard-type cashiering machines to ones that are linked to the corporate computer. I had to learn the system pretty fast, so that I could teach the rest of the crew."

"Yeah, things are changing alright.

Their meal came soon after and they carried on the conversation. Finishing desert, they left and drove back to her house. Approaching her door, Tina said, "Okay, Nathan, this was a pretty good date for me, so I'd be willing to go out again."

"It did seem nice. I have your number, so why don't I call you and we could set something up to go somewhere. Maybe you want me to meet Billy next time."

"Sure, if you want to. I do need to find out if you would be good with him before this gets too far off the ground."

"Fair enough," he said. "I'll call you later this week." Leaning closer to her, they gave each other a quick, perfunctory, almost business-like kiss. She unlocked the door as he walked away.

Several days later, he called, and they decided to have dinner at her house with Billy. Arriving on time, he had been invited in and had presented Tina with a bottle of white wine.

She had told him that they would be having Fettuccine with clam sauce and garlic bread which would go nicely with the wine.

There on the couch holding a stuffed dog toy was six-year-old Billy. He resembled Tina in coloring and being slim.

"Billy, this is Nathan, a friend of Mommy's."

"Hey Billy, how you doin'?" Nathan had two young nephews and a young niece. He was used to speaking this same way with them.

Billy looked at Nathan and said, "Hi."

"Nice dog, what's its name?"

"This is Spotty."

"Wow, fun name."

Then Tina had taken over. "Okay, guys, let's get to the table for eats."

"Yay," Billy had said.

"Looking forward to it," Nathan had said.

Sitting there, Tina and Nathan made small talk with Billy not doing much talking but concentrating on wrestling his fingers through the noodles, with several of the noodles, dripping with sauce, sliding out of his bowl and onto the table. A side of Tina that had not even been hinted at then had suddenly revealed itself.

"Billy! Stop messing with that food!" She had dropped her fork, lifted her hand, and had almost slapped Billy across his cheek.

Billy didn't react. He just stopped playing with his food and had picked up his fork again, going back to scooping up noodles as best as possible.

In that moment, Nathan had thought this must be how Tina and Billy were getting along. He had not said anything – he was too uncomfortable.

They had gone back to their conversation and had finished their meal. Tina had served ice cream for desert which Billy had enjoyed.

"Let me put Billy to bed," Tina had said, "then we can finish up."

Nathan didn't know what she had in mind, but he wasn't really feeling up to doing much else, just calling this night over.

Coming out of the bedroom, Tina had said, "Okay, now that dinner is over, is there something else you wanted?"

Nathan had hesitated a moment, thinking to himself, yes, something quite physical, just out of his loneliness. He hadn't been ready, however, to switch gears from his shock to acceptance of how Tina had treated Billy.

"Actually, Tina," he had said, "I'm thinking that maybe we just take this one moment at a time and we could go out next time somewhere fun, for you and Billy."

"Alright," she had said, ignoring the obvious tension. "I'm okay with that. "How about next time we take the train into Greenwich Village and walk around."

"I want to get a picture done of Billy and we can stop by one of the street artists for that."

"That's pretty ambitious," he had said, "but yeah, we can do that. I'm free next Saturday night, if you are."

"I'm free. I'm not working next Saturday. Let's do it. Why don't you meet me here about six o'clock and we'll travel into the city."

"Okay, I'll see you next week."

Nathan had left her apartment, only barely comfortable.

That next Saturday, Nathan had come by, and the three of them took the subway to the Village. First, they had stopped into a restaurant and had something to eat.

Then they had walked around West 4th Street with Tina looking for an artist who displayed acceptable portraits. She had decided on a particular vendor and had bargained for a reasonable price to do a quick sketch of Billy.

Nathan had watched as Billy sat for the picture, as it was now about 9:30 p.m. It was obviously late for Billy, as Nathan had watched as his eyes were drooping closed and his body had been swaying with tiredness. The portrait was completed, and they had walked to the train station and had traveled back to Tina's neighborhood, arriving about 11:30 p.m. Billy had been almost asleep, and Tina had carried him the last two blocks to their house.

Even with this demonstration of caring, Nathan had again felt uncomfortable with the way in which Tina appeared to be ignoring Billy's needs earlier in the evening.

Finishing putting Billy to bed, it had seemed to Nathan that Tina was again inviting Nathan to stay later, but he still couldn't separate his carnal craving from the episode with Billy's portrait. But he still couldn't get off the moving train.

They had left it that Nathan would come by the next weekend to see if he could help her with preparing to paint her kitchen.

She was definitely going to handle the roller and brush work, but he was being solicited to contribute hands for emptying the cabinets.

So, that next Saturday, he had come over. Billy had been deposited with Tina's mother to keep him out of the way. Nathan had then spent a few hours taking direction from Tina in dismantling the contents of the kitchen cabinets. It was at this point that he had started to envision repainting his own dismal apartment.

About five o'clock, Tina had called it quits and it was here that Nathan, too, was ready to end this ride. He had thought that he wouldn't be able to change much in Billy's life without committing to a full-blown relationship with Tina. He had not been prepared to move further in that direction.

Regardless that she had influenced his choice to make changes in his home environment, which he promised himself that he would get to, this train ride was coming to a stop.

Halloween Parties

His brother and sister-in-law had arranged this date for Jack. Divorced for two years, his successes in dating since the decree had been marginal. But this night, on Halloween, there were two costume parties to go to, and Jack would be escorting Sharon, a successful banking industry Account Executive.

Jack was the Vice-President for Marketing in his firm, a large real estate development entity, and the family thought that Sharon and Jack would be a good match. Jack's former wife had been working as a manager for a multi-state flower delivery service, and Sharon's former husband from three years ago, had been an insurance adjuster, as Jack had found out from speaking with her while putting the finishing touches on this date.

Jack's marriage had ended by mutual agreement to dissolve their union after eight years, based on different rates of personal development. It was nobody's fault; it just didn't have the same flavor as it had in the beginning and needed to be vacated.

Apparently for Sharon, and her former husband of ten years, for them it was the betrayal of an affair that she could not tolerate.

So, although Jack had been warned by his sister-in-law that her friend Sharon, while a cracker-jack banker, could be less than organized in her attention to the overall logistics of appointments and commitments, Jack, a detail-oriented purist, was hoping that all would be well on this date.

Jack had put his simple costume outfit together before this day. He had devised a complement of a sweater vest with the arms of a second shirt that he had stuffed with crumpled newspapers, slipped through the vest under his own arms, and then he had topped it off with gardening gloves baste-stitched onto the cuffs — yes, he was now the four-armed monster. So clever, he thought.

Sharon had told him that she was going to be wearing a ballerina-type outfit, so that she would be a princess. His sister-in-law, a successful civil attorney, was dressing as the bride of Dracula, while his brother, one of the principal owners of a commercial renovation firm, would be sporting a tuxedo which he owned outright and was going as Dracula. Not bad for two couples in their late thirties. Whoopie.

Jack and Sharon had made up to meet near Jack's brother's house a few miles outside of New York City to save some extra driving in traffic.

They were going first to an upscale club where they expected to have cocktails, and to socialize with several of his sister-in-law's associates, among other members of the business community.

Following some time at the club, they were committed to then joining another party some distance away that would be populated by friends of Jack's brother. There was no thought that they would not attend both functions. Too many promises had been made in order to network with each of the other's enterprises. It sounded like a reasonable plan, although not perfect.

And the evening did not get off to a good start. Jack received the first call from Sharon about three hours before they were to meet. She had apparently misplaced her car keys and was waiting for an auto locksmith to get her going again. Jack called his sister-in-law to give her the news. Then he waited for the update.

Sharon called him after about an hour. The locksmith was there, and she was expecting to get on the road shortly. Jack drove to his brother's house in anticipation of gathering to head to the club.

Sharon arrived at the house running about a half-hour late. Not too bad, thought Jack, considering the circumstances that Sharon had to face this afternoon.

Here she was, though, an attractive woman of medium height with brown hair cut short, dark eyes, nicely accentuated with a carefully-made up face wearing a ballerina outfit under a light jacket. A nice package thought Jack, and he dismissed the demerits on time management that he had been contemplating.

Jack, also of medium build with blonde hair, blue eyes, and wearing his gentle monster clothes was seemingly acceptable to Sharon. Dracula and his bride completed the ensemble. They climbed into his brother's car and drove to the club.

It was a nicely-decorated bar displaying a full complement of Halloween extravaganza. They found a table nearby to several friends. Jack volunteered to get drinks for Sharon and himself with the idea to test out his second set of arms. Walking up to the bar, he placed his right-stuffed gloved arm in front of the bartender and ordered two gin and tonics. Satisfactorily for Jack, the bartender did a slight double-take and grinned.

There were plenty of other costumed individuals at the bar, and in the club, so while it was not a complete surprise that a four-armed creature would be walking up to the bar, it was certainly a treat.

Jack carried the drinks back to the table with two of his real arms and joined in the active conversation. As this was Sharon and Jack's first date, they certainly needed to get to know one another.

They continued this process in earnest from their conversation which started during their drive to the club. Things seemed to be going well, and they had a second set of drinks.

Their interlude was far too short, though. They were reminded that it was time to leave for the other party. Sharon and Jack were disappointed to be going, but they had known that they were doing this to respect the obligation.

Fitting themselves back in the car, they drove to a town just on the other side of the Hudson River in New Jersey. This party was at a friend's house without the sophistication of a public bar.

Walking in, they were greeted warmly by friends, and proceeded to mingle slightly before Jack and Sharon slipped away to a corner of the large living room.

Securing drinks, they chatted amiably throughout the rest of the evening, and discovered many similarities in their lives, both before, during and after their previous marriages.

At one point, Jack even placed one of his fake arms on Sharon's leg, and she smiled.

Coming on to about 1:00 a.m., the group decided to call it a night. They drove back to pick up Sharon's car. Although it was late, Jack was bold enough to suggest to her that they could perhaps share a nightcap, at either of their apartments.

Sharon was bold enough to agree, recommending her place, and had her own suggestion that they would need to change out of their costumes into something more comfortable.

Jack was in accord with this idea but doubted that comfortable attire would be required for very long while attending a private third party on this charming Halloween night. He had no intention of using anything but his own real arms for the rest of the evening.

The Meeting

It was Thanksgiving Day, 1983, but not altogether a day to give thanks. Since roasting a dead animal is associated with this holiday, Blake Shearing had thought it appropriate the night before that he should stick his head in the oven. Sticking his head in the oven was just one scenario that had revealed itself among other considerations of death methodologies.

Blake, a licensed civil engineer, had been terribly alone for the past three years since his wife Mallory of twenty-two years had decided to pursue another interest of hers. She had met a man at a business conference and had kept up an affair with him for a very long time. After all the years invested in their marriage, Blake had to deal with the rending of this partnership by divorce and had not adjusted very well at all. They did not have children, so there was no one in the immediate family unit that he could commiserate with if he had chosen to do so.

During those years after the breakup, he had dated occasionally, once that had led to a second date, and on two occasions he had had dates which led to furtive, temporary, meaningless sex, however, with no tangible electricity from these unions, there would be no attachments.

The date that he had been on the weekend before Thanksgiving had been arranged by a mutual friend. Although he thought that the prospect and he might be attracted to each other, it was basically one-sided, on each of their parts.

Although they engaged in some meaningful conversation, all they had finally shared was the discomfort of their loneliness.

It was with particular courage that he had permitted his friend to provide him with the name and phone number of this possible merger – Sandra Mathis. As his friend provided background, she was a woman about Blake's age, and divorced for several years after a marriage of nineteen years. She had two teenage children.

Blake called her and they were going to meet on a Friday evening in the lobby of the building where she worked as a designer for a furniture manufacturer.

He stood in the lobby, neatly dressed in a blue sports jacket, gray slacks, and a maroon tie as they had arranged, so that she could identify him. His close-cropped dark hair was streaked with gray, and complemented his dark brown eyes and clean-shaven face. His features were strong, but understated, with a well-balanced nose spacing the area between moderately full lips. He was solidly-built, 6'-1" in height and certainly looked like he could take care of himself.

His emotional state, however, was such that he was just barely hanging on to equilibrium. He was determined to convince Sandra that he was as solid and stable mentally as he looked physically.

He was anticipating her to be wearing a blue suit and a red blouse, as they had also agreed, since he wouldn't have otherwise recognized her.

He saw her. She looked his way and they acknowledged each other with a quick, affirmative nod.

She was at once vaguely pretty, almost beautiful, but oddly so, that one might view her features as a little too peculiar to call lovely but nonetheless perceiving that she was.

Having a too-round nose that missed matching the somewhat thin and oblong delicacy of her smooth, undefined cheeks, and showing a straight-across mouth even as she mildly smiled, interrupted calling her beautiful. She displayed large, dark blue eyes and wore her dark, curly hair short, but full at the top, over her ears and landing at her neck.

Walking up to him, her face reaching his mouth, Sandra looked up and stated, "Blake? I'm Sandra."

"Hello Sandra," extending his hand, "Nice to meet you," he said somewhat rigidly.

She moved back a step. Watching as she looked him over, he did not get the impression that she was any too keen on this meeting. From the several dates that he had been on, he was well aware that if there was no link within the first ten seconds, there was little chance of further development.

In fact, his telephone conversation with Sandra to set up this meeting had been rather tentative; both knowing that this forced rendezvous was just that — forced by a well-meaning friend.

Standing in the lobby, without much enthusiasm, but hanging on to convention, Sandra said, "I know a place down the street where we can get a drink. Do you want to do that?"

"Fine," he answered flatly.

She led the way through the revolving doors of the building and turned toward their destination. Entering the bar, they isolated a table for themselves, sat opposite each other and ordered cocktails.

Blake said, "You know, I was reluctant to actually keep this date. From how you sounded on the phone, I could tell that you could probably have skipped this evening."

Sandra leaned back and looked at him. "Well, that was the way I felt since I'm never too sure if any of this is worth it. As I told you, I was married for a long time and haven't been interested in pursuing a second career in that field, though, I have been out a few times with different people."

"Well, like I told you," Blake said, leaning slightly forward, "I was married, too, for a long time, but it fell apart which also took a long time. I thought my wife and I had this dream marriage, but some of the unstable things in it, like our reservations about gluing ourselves to each other, were enough to make it disintegrate. I've tried some dating, but like you say, it mostly doesn't work too well."

"Well, I was in shock from my breakup," Sandra said. "It happened pretty quickly."

"Even though I was married for a long time, since my ex-husband was a completely selfish and self-absorbed man, it was only the illusion of our happiness that couldn't possibly sustain itself."

She took a sip of her drink and continued, "After we were divorced, and once I started to regain my sanity, I could see that I didn't want to put myself in that position again."

Blake leaned in closer. "It doesn't have to be that way again. You could meet someone who could help you get rid of those notions." He was grasping at straws here.

"Like you, for instance?" she retorted - not sarcastically, just factually.

"Well, I don't know, Sandra, we just met," as he leaned away. "I wouldn't think that you could jump ship at a moment's notice from your paradigm, not even for me, but it could happen." This proposal was a very positive stretch for Blake since he was really feeling just low enough to be playing handball in the street against the curb, or to be having a tag match with a pebble.

"No, you're right," she mused, folding her hands. "It couldn't be that simple. I'm just barely comfortable sitting here with you. Thinking about taking this anywhere else would be a real surprise for me — and I'm guessing for you too."

"I can't disagree with you there. I might be hoping, yes," he lied, then continued, "but my experiences have led me to have some pretty grim observations about human behavior. Sometimes, my view of the world concerns me."

"That's like me," Sandra countered. "Even though I was discarded by my ex, I was losing something valuable to me which was excruciatingly sad. It was a painful, lethal dose of reality."

"That's the way it was for me," Blake said. "My marriage demanded to be thrown away, even though it defined me. I needed a special strength to respond to what was for me this enormous tragedy. I didn't handle it very well. I drifted as a wandering generality for a long time, and even though I think that I am presenting a firm persona, I'm still in crazy time, to reference that current book *Crazy Time* by Abigail Trafford."

"I do know what you mean, and I can appreciate that," she said. "I was devastated and lost since I understood myself as a married woman and a mother, even though it was kind of unbalanced, but at least, I felt like I 'belonged' in society. I picked up that book, too — very popular in these days of divorcing and people killing themselves over it."

"Something like Dr. Kubler-Ross' *Perspectives on Death and Dying* with all those various stages and other insights. I didn't think that I would connect with someone anytime soon, and even now, it's just not happening for me. Do you have children?" she asked, changing the subject.

"No, we never did get to that. We tried several times, but it just didn't materialize, so we gave up."

"That's too bad," she said. "I guess if you had, maybe you'd still be together – no, let me take that back. I should know better. My marriage breaking up just didn't have anything to do with children, one way or the other."

"You're right" Blake said. "None of this has anything to do with children. I can imagine, though, that you having children during the mess of your marriage ending must have been really hard."

"It was, but not as much on me as it was so much more on them. Even though their father wasn't totally there for them either, he was still their father, and they were affected by the loss."

"That's too bad," he said. "I feel sorry for them, but hope they can recover, and that you can be there for them."

"You can still be their mom, even though you see yourself outside of the world, not belonging to it as an unmarried parent."

"I guess I could see it that way," she said. "So, how about you belonging in society?" she asked. "How did you feel about that?"

"Well, for me," Blake sighed, "I wanted to find someone again, and thought that I would, since I missed the intimacy of what could be found in a relationship, even though it had been gone in my marriage for a while. But I still wanted that companionship, not only for the mental part, but let's face it, to be physical."

"Well for me," Sandra said plaintively, "I did have some intimacy in the early days of my marriage, and I did like that, and we were having sex, but when it started to fade, I gave up trying to enjoy myself. Now I just don't think about it much, or don't face it, anyway."

They looked directly at each other. There was no mistaking that there would not be any additional bonding beyond exchanging these words in this discussion. They finished their drinks in silence.

"I don't think we're ordering anything else, are we?" Blake asked.

"I don't think so," Sandra said. "I know we had an intense conversation and all that, but like I said, I'm not sure that I can confront these evenings of soul-searching confessions."

"Well, you and I were both spilling out with some inner thoughts here," Blake said, "but if we're done, we're done. I'm ready to call it an evening."

"Thanks for understanding, Blake, maybe some other time," she said drearily.

"Maybe, Sandra, but I'm almost counting on this being our only meeting for some time."

"I think we need to keep it that way," she said.

"What about the holiday? Are you spending it with anyone?" he asked.

"My children, a few relatives, not much of anything," she said. "How about you?"

"I'm seeing my mother and my sister's family, and some assorted relatives. I guess it will be okay."

"Well, I suppose we have to keep on going," she said.

"Yeah, I suppose. Okay if I pay this check?" he asked.

"If you want. Thanks."

They walked to the door and out to the street.

"Nice to meet you, Sandra, please take care of yourself," he said quietly.

"You, too, Blake, sorry for your troubles," she said sympathetically.

"Yeah, me too," he said in resignation. "Too bad about your challenges."

They shook hands, then she turned and walked away. He went in the opposite direction.

Thanksgiving, indeed, thought Blake.

Pinewood Derby

Johnathan's wife Deborah had been dead for three years, having struggled with an aggressive cancer. As the Cub Master for his nine-year old son David's pack, however, he still maintained the commitment to attend the Tuesday evening meetings, bringing his son to join in with his den of five scouts, the rest of the boys in the pack, and letting his seven-year old daughter Coreen mingle either with children who were there with the other scout families, or with the fledging Brownie troop that had recently been formed.

His wife had also been active in Scouting, working with the older boys during the meetings, and pitching-in with the Brownies as needed. The boys in the pack missed Deborah, and the girls missed her. David and Coreen were somewhat becoming used to her not being in their lives, but Johnathan was not doing very well at all.

Focusing on bringing up his son and daughter on his own, with the help of their former day-care provider when needed, and while they were in school, took the edge from the tasks, but he was still in the framework of worry and concern.

And he had become increasingly lonely for adult companionship. He needed someone who he could talk to more often than with other Scout leaders just on Tuesday evenings, or with his co-workers as an architectural Auto Cad designer for a small consulting firm.

His life with Deborah and the children had been full and satisfying. If he could replicate that with someone new, in a meaningful, committed relationship, he felt that he could move forward. Johnathon was thirty-six years old, of medium height with dark hair, neatly cut. He was an emotional person whose feelings were readily demonstrated.

In the world of Scouting, the limits to meeting new people were confined to the current group of adult leaders, who were either parents of the scouts in the pack and troop, or grandparents of same, but in any case, many seemed to be in on-going relationships. All the members of the adult group had been devastated by the loss of Deborah, and they were as kind and sympathetic as they could be, but her loss was also fading into their memories for these adults, and there wasn't much that they could do for Johnathan.

Then an opportunity came around for him to meet someone new at an annual event.

This year, as in past years, the scouts were going to participate in the district-wide Pinewood Derby. While Johnathon had participated in this recurring venue during the past three years, he had not been feeling up to recognizing a connection with someone.

The Derby, a distinctive scouting enterprise, involved the pack purchasing the inexpensive kits for each boy which contained a seven-inch long rectangular pine block, two steel axles, and four plastic wheels.

The project involved building and decorating a model of a racing car, then competing against other scouts with these cars on a gravity track with trophies awarded to winners in different classes of age and rank. The Cub Scouts in these competitions were aged seven to eleven years old.

First, each blank car was prepared by one of the other scout leaders by cutting it to a basic streamlined shape using a table-saw. Once they were dressed this way, they were ready for assembling and painting.

There were strict rules against enhancing the cars with any friction-defeating features that would provide advantages over other scouts' cars, and they all had weight limits within specified parameters.

While extra decorations were permitted, the addition of driver figures or other enhancements would add to the weight and needed to be carefully considered.

The overall weight of the cars, at the official five-ounce limit, was adjusted before race day as needed by the sophisticated adding of pennies glued to their undersides, then they were checked at the track by other volunteer scout leaders with precision scales.

It was a key factor that the boys were to work on their cars without the assistance of adults. Although it was hoped that adults would not put too much effort into taking over the project, sometimes they did. Johnathan wanted David to work on the car by himself and controlled his urge to jump in physically to help with placing the axles in the pre-cut slots in the wood block, mounting the wheels on the axles, then designing and executing the paint scheme.

David seemed to be working well on his own, and Johnathan did not see a reason to provide hands-on intervention.

The racing event was held at the local shopping mall. There in one of the main concourses, district Scout leaders set up the forty-foot long multi-rowed track, at an inclined height of four feet from the starting gate to the level finish line.

These days the district had purchased an electronic device to determine first, second, and third place winners, eliminating the potential, and sometimes realized, ugliness of disputes fostered by adults over finishers.

With about one-hundred Cub Scouts from a half-dozen packs weighing-in to qualify in their divisions, the area around the track was a vision of lightly-controlled pandemonium. Also included were at least more than that number of adults who had brought their Cubs to the race.

The Cubs had placed their cars for display on several nearby tables. Scout Leader judges evaluated the cars' paint schemes, decorations, and shapes for originality and uniqueness for presentation of selected awards. The aerodynamics would be determined at race time. Participants and their adult supervisors were excited and nervous pending the outcome of judging and racing. While some of the Cubs may have been more worried than others, it likely did not compare to the uncertainties of the adults. This was supposed to be a fun event, but placing adults into the mix could be a stressful combination.

Johnathon was not apprehensive. He was not overly concerned about the outcome of the race, nor was David especially competitive, but Johnathon was not totally comfortable.

He couldn't help that more often than not, he was distracted by his thinking of what he would be facing following the day's activities.

Home with the children, fixing dinner, getting them ready for school on Monday, and the inevitable staring at the television screen, or reading, silently, until going to work the next morning.

While his son and daughter had scrambled off to play with other Scout children and siblings in another area of the mall until the race started, there was a moment standing near his son's car at one of the tables when Johnathon couldn't help noticing a woman standing near him, also looking at the cars. She was a light-haired woman of medium build, and like Johnathon, was wearing a Scout uniform.

Moving closer to him, she pointed to one of the cars and said, "That's my son Joseph's car. Does your son have one here?" she asked.

Johnathon gulped slightly, pointed and answered, "Yes, my son David's is that bluish-orange one over there. What pack are you with?" he asked.

"Oh, we're with three-ninety-two over in Canarsie. How about you?" she asked

"We're here with four-fourteen from Midwood. How many Cubs in your pack?"

"We're about twelve strong, with a WEBELOS group of five transitioning to Scouts. How many do you have?"

"We've got nine Wolfs through Bears, with six WEBELOS, and then on the Troop side we have more than fifteen Scouts, plus our leadership. My name's Johnathon and I'm the Cub Master over there. What do you do in your pack?"

She turned her face toward him, and he noticed clear, blue eyes. "I'm Wynona, and I'm the Den Leader and Treasurer. For the past two years," she said, "I've been keeping up with these responsibilities, but since Joseph's father left us when Joseph was eight, it's been a stretch to stay focused. I'm thirty-two and can maintain the effort, but I have to work at it, and concentrate at my nursing job. Thank goodness Joseph is playing right now with some other Cubs."

"You're a nurse? Where do you do that?"

"I've been with the Methodist Hospital in Park Slope for quite a while. Lots of hard work and crazy hours."

"That does seem like much on your plate. Too bad about your husband," Johnathon said. "Does he come around at all?"

"No, that's really the trouble. It's only me who's maintaining Joseph in the Pack. He likes it, but he's been confused about his disappeared dad. Our marriage hadn't been so good for a while, then he took off. I have another child as well, Joseph's sister Dorothy, who's twelve. She's at my mom's house today for the race. How about you? Is your wife involved in Scouting?"

Johnathon was surprised that Wynona was opening up to him so easily, but he just focused on responding.

"That's really the trouble with me," Johnathon said. "My wife died a few years ago and I've got the children. My son David, who's nine, and his sister Coreen, who's seven, just like your son Joseph are off playing right now with the other children waiting for the race to start."

"That's too bad about your wife. I'm sorry. As a special-care nurse, I see all kinds of heartbreak. How bad has it been with the two children?"

"Well, not so bad with them, it's just been kind of sad being without my partner, but I've been managing."

"My design job keeps me concentrating on work, but it's been a struggle. How about you? Without your husband and on your own, how has that been?"

"Oh, you design things? Is that in fashion or something else?"

"In the building trades," he answered.

"That's interesting," she said, then went on. "Well, since it was only barely functioning for some time, I don't miss former husband too much, but I have been missing a close friend. Being in the Scouting family works only so much, if you know what I mean."

"I know all too well what you mean. It's friendly, and sociable, but there's that missing factor of, well, seems like I'm preaching to the choir here."

"Yeah, you seem to get it," she said. "Are you looking to make a new friend, or something like that?" she asked.

Johnathon hesitated for the briefest second. "I am interested in pursuing this conversation," he said. "Why don't we get the children back over here for the race, then if I can get your number we could meet sometime soon."

"That sounds nice," she said. "Here's to our Cubs on winning or coming in second, or even third."

"Yes, to a good race," Johnathon said. And not since in some time had he felt like he might be moving out of this track's pit stop alley and approaching a lap towards the winner's circle.

Brighter Nights

It was always night for Alex in those days when he was working the 4:00 p.m. to 12:00 a.m. shift in the engine room. He was three levels below the street at a large office building in New York City. He was a licensed Refrigeration Operating Engineer, responsible for running the behemoth steam turbine-driven commercial air conditioning machines located in the lower depths of this building. Fading light as winter approached when he started his shift, it was completely dark when he left at midnight, then home to prepare a meal, and then falling into some restless sleep before beginning the cycle again

He was thirty-five years old, and recently divorced from a ten-year marriage. How he had been married and was then divorced with no children was a long story following his discharge from the U.S. Army, but he was moving on from this history.

During the long hours at work, he had determined that his marriage with Veronica had failed because he just hadn't put the effort into granting to her the space that she needed to grow in the direction where she was headed.

She was in increasingly responsible administrative leadership positions in the emerging computer industry.

He was rooted in the analog world of bulky, loud, and greasy mechanisms. While she was personally changing to meet the challenges of digital electronics and customer service, he was maintaining his competency in the world of archaic, though completely functional, mechanical apparatuses.

Although he thought about these things, he also knew that his increasing focus on the basic core values of Christianity and ethics did not match her more ambitious attitudes about the business world which prevented her from recognizing the spirituality of everyday life. Their communications with, and understandings of, each other had become more infrequent until these episodes had disappeared completely.

Prior to securing his night shift position, he had been working during the day only one level beneath the sidewalk as an Operating Engineer at a local university, responsible for similar, but electric-driven machines. It was relatively peaceful there, with regular hours that contributed to a quiet married life in the evenings after work.

While he went home regularly, Veronica's schedule was becoming more erratic which isolated her from their relationship.

She wasn't making up for the time spent away from home, and he was doing nothing to sympathize with her business choices. He scrubbed the grease from his hands and began to attend church every Sunday, while she stayed at home to catch up on proposals and purchase orders, and the development of networks. She did not appreciate Alex's more mundane and static work-life choice.

It was the mid-nineteen eighties. Soon after the divorce, he had changed jobs for more money and went on the night shift. Now, these two years later, he signed on with a dating service, a somewhat popular venue at the time, in order to meet prospective soul-mate women. Since he was basically hidden amongst the machines during the evenings, dating in the conventional method just wasn't successful.

Registering with the service, basic factors of age, height, weight, and other personal, social and philosophical preferences were provided to the intake representative. No pictures were viewed by prospective daters.

Through the service, he met single women, distant women, and superficial women. Then he met Candice.

He had followed procedures and called her, sight unseen.

The phone rang twice. "Candice, this is Alex, I believe you're expecting my call?"

"Yes, hello. I got the message from the service. This is a little strange to be doing this, but it's the modern way, right?"

"Yeah, I know what you mean. I haven't called anyone like this for quite a while. I've been divorced for a couple of years and didn't do it this way when I started dating. But you probably knew from my background info that I'm divorced."

"Yes, I read your bio. I'm divorced too, as you know. I've been divorced for the past three years, and you know that my son is seven years old. Does that scare you off?"

"No, not at all. I knew that you were a mom. I'm an uncle. I have one niece and one nephew. What's your son's name?"

"He's Danny. Well, really Daniel, but we never called him anything else but Danny. You don't sound like you mind, but I didn't see that you had children – you don't, right?"

"No. Like I said, I'm an uncle for my niece and nephew who are still little."

"I always liked being their uncle and maybe my ex-wife and I might have started to have children, but we never got around to it."

"Yeah, you never know about those things," she said. "My ex and I went pretty much right at it and had Danny. I'm sure you know all too well that we can't go back again. We have to live how it is now."

"Well," he said, "That kind of thinking took me a while to get to. I don't know about you, but I never thought that my wife and I couldn't work out our differences until we just couldn't work them out, and then it was over."

"Well, for me," she said, "I thought I was in love, and that my husband loved me. Then my marriage fell apart real quick when he began sneaking off with this other woman. Before you know it, he abandoned me and our son. It was ugly and a really bad time in my life. I couldn't move forward for a long time from those first raw months. It took me more than two years when I started to recover that I could step back into the social circle by using this dating service."

"Candice, I know the feeling. Here I was as an engineer on this track of watching gauges, supervising the steady rumble of a smooth-running mechanical plant."

"Then I had no purpose or sharing with another human being. Well, no close relationship, anyway. Fortunately, I had the Church, so I wasn't completely alone, just dangling."

"I know you said that in your write-up that you attend church. And you said that you're an engineer. That's something neat, to be able to mix religion and science," she said.

"Not really much of a stretch," he said. "After all, everything comes from God, right?"

"Okay, I'll go along with you on that for the time being."

"Fair enough. How about you? You said in your write-up that you were working as an office manager in a back-office setting for a kitchen appliance manufacturer. That's some technical stuff. You didn't mention that you were in a church, though."

"No, actually the work that I'm doing is just basic administrative things and maintaining the financial side of the business. I'm not out there on the factory floor, but I do know how our products are put together and shipped out. As far as religion, I didn't have much of it when I was growing up, but I really need to start thinking about what I should be doing for Danny at this age."

"Well, I tell you what, Candice. Since we really don't know each other very well, why don't I just invite you out on a first date to maybe see a movie or maybe just have some coffee, and we can see where this goes from there?"

"Alright, Alex. I'm free this next Saturday night about seven o'clock when I would ask my mother to watch Danny. We could just meet to have a bite to eat, and we'll see where we're going."

"That's fine. I know where you live, but if you want, we could meet somewhere and take it from there."

"No, it's okay. After all, the dating service has cleared us from being criminals. Why don't you pick me up at my house, since you know where I am, and I know that you don't live too far anyway. We can go to the Concord Diner on Neptune Avenue. You know where that is?" she asked.

"Sounds great. I know where that is. So, I'll see you next Saturday at seven o'clock. It's been nice talking with you tonight."

"Yes, it was nice even though we talked about some of our dark past," she said.

"Well, you know, it could be like that when you start a conversation with someone new."

"And we're just starting this new conversation."

"Sure, but now this new one won't have that same edge when we meet in person," he said.

"That sounds good. I'll see you Saturday."

"Good night, Candice."

"So long, Alex."

It was Saturday. Alex approached Candice's apartment and rang the bell. She opened the door and said, "Hello, Alex. Won't you come in?"

He stepped across the threshold to stand in a small foyer. Seeing her for the first time, she was slightly shorter than him, was slim with short blonde hair, dark blue eyes, and was casually dressed.

"Please come in." He stepped past her. She closed the door. They shook hands.

"Nice to meet you," Alex said.

"Nice to meet you, too," Candice said.

She led him through the foyer into the living room and asked him to sit on the couch.

"We won't stay but a bit," she said. "Let me get my bag and we'll go."

Alex looked around the room. It was plainly furnished with contemporary furniture.

She returned from a bedroom. Alex stood up. He could see her sizing him up, a fair-complexioned man of average height, with light brown hair, green eyes, dressed in neat, casual attire.

Leaving the apartment, they walked to Alex's car that was parked around the corner.

"Not always easy to park round here," she said. "Sometimes, I drive around several times before I find a spot."

"Well, it wasn't too bad," he said. "Not any worse than where I live."

"That's the city for you. Plenty of noise and stress but not a lot of parking spaces. It's just something we have to live with. I'm not too fussy since I take the train to work and can just leave my car during the week, and don't see that changing anytime soon. I like my job and I'm glad to have it. As long as Danny has a safe place to play, and a decent school to go to, that's all I really care about."

"Is there somewhere nearby for that?"

"Just the next block over, there's a really nice park with slides, swings, and a sprinkler. I take him there after school when we can and on weekends too, when we can. His school is just a couple of blocks over from there."

By this time, they were traveling in Alex's car towards the restaurant. Alex listened to Candice and was impressed with her demeanor. She appeared forthright, was specific in her needs, that is, to adequately provide for her son, and seemed only moderately ambitious. She was satisfied to continue in her relatively un-stressful position with a steady paycheck.

"I have a similar situation," he said. "I take the train to work in the city and leave my car on the block. It's a nuisance with alternate side parking, but I make it happen. Unless something really drastic happens, I don't see myself changing jobs, maybe just changing shifts."

"That must be a little strange," she said. "Working on the night shift like that. I don't think that I could do it for very long. I'm more conventional in my hours."

"Well, it was a little bizarre when I first went on nights, but I was caught up in the destruction of my marriage and accepted taking on those subterranean blues. It doesn't have to stay that way. I'm almost beginning to see the light of day."

"I felt buried myself," Candice said. "I know you know how I felt because it was that way for me when I got divorced."

"I didn't see any hope and kept myself behind huge piles of paperwork on my desk. It was dark in there. It's just been these past couple of months that I started to clear those things up and contacted the dating service. Who knows? Maybe I will eventually get all of that off my desk and things will be brighter."

"Well, Candice, the way you're talking is really the way I'm feeling since we last spoke, and especially this evening."

"It does seem to be a bright spot tonight, doesn't it?"

"Thanks, Candice. That makes me feel good."

They arrived at the diner and talked about many worldly things and spiritual matters during their light meal, before returning to Candice's building.

Walking in the street Candice said, "I had a very nice time tonight, Alex."

"It was really pleasant in the scheme of things," he agreed. "I'd like to try this again really soon. If you want, we could go out again maybe next Saturday during the day if you want, and we could do something with Danny."

"That is such a nice thing for you to suggest, Alex. That would really be fun for Danny. I know - how about we head over to the Aquarium at Coney Island? We could walk around and see the fish and talk."

"That would do it, Candice. Sounds like a plan. I can give you a call later this week and we'll make up when to go. How's that?"

"I like that. So, thanks again for tonight and we'll talk."

Then, they couldn't seem to help it – they leaned into each other and kissed a quick, but warm kiss.

Beginning the next week, Alex was receptive to sharing Candice with her son. Their first time at the Aquarium was special for Danny. He loved it and didn't mind being with Alex. He had been very young when Candice had divorced her husband, and Danny's father just wasn't in his life. Alex, however, did not encroach on Candice's bond with Danny.

Sometimes, Candice would arrange for her mother to take care of Danny while she and Alex went on dates, basically on Saturday or Sunday afternoons, after church, which Alex attended on his own.

Not a particularly religious woman but recognizing that it was time to have her son exposed to the comforts of the church, after three months of dating Alex she accepted his invitation to join him there at a nearby Methodist church.

Alex introduced Candice and Danny to several of his friends and to their pastor while at the service.

Danny even joined the Sunday school group for their hour-long session and enjoyed himself with the other children. Candice seemed relaxed in the friendly atmosphere of this congregation. Now more familiar with each other, leaving church, Alex and Danny would walk ahead of Candice down the block to a bakery where they sold ice cream. The two of them would look in the case to select something, then they would sit together at a small table with Candice, talking and having fun while they ate.

"What do you think about this," Alex would joke with Danny. "Why didn't the skeleton cross the road?" Danny and Candice would look at each other.

"Why's that?" Danny asked.

"No guts!" Alex said. The two of them would laugh out loud because it was so silly.

For the next several months, the three of them would spend Sunday mornings at church, then they would have lunch, and then dinner either at Alex's or Candice's apartment, or they would go out. Danny and Alex were easy with each other, as was Alex and Candice.

The emotional toll of being hurt by their previous marital relationships seemed to be diminishing as they became increasingly intimate and loving, and knowledgeable about each of their feelings and goals.

With Candice's mother providing periodic overnight care for Danny, Alex and Candice were able to spend more private time together.

Within two years of meeting, they made their commitments to each other and were married at the church. They found a new place to live as a family, but not before Alex switched to the day shift, in line with Candice's more regular hours.

Alex did not have to wrestle with Candice's career objectives since she had expressed her satisfaction in reaching her level of competency and involvement, and it was none of Alex's affair to provide anything other than encouragement and acceptance of Candice's life choices. She was available to sustain her commitment to Danny, and now, to include Alex.

She understood and valued his steady, uneventful but satisfying career path, and they spent their quiet evenings together. In addition to a warm home life, they, along with Danny, were also in the nurturing embrace of the church.

If Alex had not been working those lonely nights, he and Candice's lives would not have become immeasurably enriched in the light of day.

Industrial Archeological

Evan Maldonado stood at the top of the stairs leading to the building's engine room three levels below the street. It was his first day on the job, after successfully interviewing for this position, as one of four of the operating engineers at this plant in a commercial office building.

He was thirty-five years old, and ten years out of the military following a fairly non-stressful period in the Army, being discharged as a Sergeant, and then working steadily following that in various mechanical trades.

He was looking forward to this next period in his life. He was well-trained, responsible, and had taken formal class instruction and training to transition from being a general mechanic to securing his municipal license to operate large commercial refrigeration equipment. He, along with others who had passed the strict written and practical license examination, had been referred to the Operating Engineers union to interview for open positions in New York City. He had been offered a day shift running the machinery in this large building.

He was also coming out of a hard divorce following six years of being married to a woman who just wanted more out of life than what Evan relished, that of a stable, quiet, pastime in a committed relationship.

Her ambitions in the world of fashion design just didn't include Evan tagging along in the background.

Following the break-up, and after struggling through a year of second-guessing, and lamenting this loss, he would be transitioning from his caste as a general mechanic earning moderate wages to the relatively high-paying level of a specialized plant watch engineer, as a member of a select profession, with a strong union.

Unfortunately, he was distracted in the triumph of this career milestone by his isolation. The divorce had taken a great deal of energy out of him, and he was still recovering. One of the lowest points in the process had been the day when he was offered the engineering position. Although this was a great accomplishment in his career, his loneliness left him standing in his apartment that evening, crying that he had no one meaningful with whom to share this news.

He resisted against staying in this depth of hopelessness and refocused on what he had achieved in his career.

That same evening, while he was soon to enter the depths of the engine room, he made a conscious decision to resist against the desolation of his failed marriage, and to rise again into the world of human contact.

And as sometimes happens, it started on its own. Traveling on the subway to that first day on the job, he was sitting in a train car next to three women who seemed about his age. They were dressed casually, though fashionably.

He was dressed simply in a pocket tee-shirt, khaki work pants, wearing his steel-toed black boots, and he carried a small duffel bag with his lunch. Anticipating his arrival in the next half-hour at the new job, but still in his shady gloom, he did not think of himself as desirable.

But at least one of the women obviously must have thought so. He heard her say coquettishly to her companions, "Be still my heart." There was no mistaking her statement being directed to him. Way too shy to respond, he just continued to stare across the train car aisle, immobile, but this one flicker of light had registered in his mind.

They left the train at the next station, and Evan could continue his journey towards the engine room, fragile emotions still in place.

His skills would be put to the test in the harsh environment of the lower complexities of this office building. Constructed in 1925, and now sixty-years old, the plant contained steam turbine and electric-driven refrigeration machines, providing air conditioning throughout the building.

The steam was provided from the utility company through underground piping from the street, at one-hundred-fifty pounds per square inch, then it was stepped down through reducing valves to run the turbines.

The turbines were coupled to compressors that created an extremely low pressure in a sealed vessel, where liquid refrigerant that was piped through it would absorb heat from surrounding water, lowering the temperature of this now-chilled water, which was pumped through coils of tubing.

With air blown across these coils, the cooled air was distributed by fans throughout ductwork to individual offices. Monitoring the operation of the machines and their auxiliary equipment was critical to maintaining the low enough temperature of the chilled water to provide air conditioning. The water ideally needed to be held to a temperature of less than forty-five degrees for best system efficiency.

Producing water at a higher temperature than forty-five degrees would affect the ability to provide low enough air temperatures in office spaces for adequate cooling. And, producing water at a temperature approaching freezing at thirty-two degrees, while a difficult process, could result in catastrophic destruction of these chillers. Evan was completely competent at maintaining the plant within these established parameters.

There were numerous controls, gauges, valves, pumps, electrical panels, motors, and the building's elevator equipment located in the engine room that Evan was responsible for monitoring and repairing as necessary.

Evan would need to become familiar with the specific equipment in this space, but he was well acquainted with the basics of operation, maintenance, and repair of these machines.

At the age of this installation, while the core technology had not changed in more than a half century, the vintage system and individual elements would demand his full attention and care for this antiquated equipment. Some of this equipment was operated by leather belts connected to electric motors, akin to nineteenth-century mechanics. This was very old. More modern equipment uses direct-drive couplings.

Besides operating the plant, beginning on Saturday mornings, with split days off on Sunday, then Tuesday, he would also be scheduled to work a weekly shift once a month in the elevator shop located adjacent to the engine room.

Since the engine room was below the elevator pits, he would need to climb the stairs out of that space to access the passenger and freight cars, shafts, and overhead machinery for the hydraulic and traction elevator banks. Carrying a tool belt with an assortment of typical and specialized tools, and a pocket notebook, he would be responsible for trouble-shooting failed equipment, and for the harrowing responsibility of getting passengers out of stopped cars.

He would need some on-the-job training for this aspect of his engineering assignment, but he would be working with another technician who had been servicing these elevators for many years.

While the mechanical basics and techniques were unchanged since the construction of this building, the equipment had its peculiarities of operation that would also require his dedicated attention.

The next several months were filled, for example, with learning the piping and valve systems in the plant, and the requirements necessary to operate, and repair elevators.

He would be faced with the nuances of starting and monitoring air compressors, operating large and small pumps, and running the behemoth steam turbines.

These machines required respect in performing the correct sequence of operations for admitting live steam, exhausting it, and maintaining the correct speed as identified by their vibrating tachometers. More modern equipment in other plants had different methods of operations, but these antiques required their own set of established procedures.

There were other things to be done as well. A particularly precise task one day involved the need to replace the packing on the shaft of a sixty-year-old sump pump. Packing material is soft and flexible and is wrapped in rings around a pump shaft so that the shaft can rotate while maintaining a seal against the liquid being pumped.

There are no mistakes permitted in how the packing material needs to be cut at an angle, and overlapped around the shaft, and how tightly the packing gland needs to be adjusted.

A vital and expensive piece of equipment could easily fail if the work is not performed correctly by a qualified mechanic, technician, or an engineer.

Now the sump, which collected condensate and other drainage from the plant, was located below the engine room. This was a hellish location, dark, wet, and populated by animal life of all sorts.

Evan had encountered many kinds of vermin in many areas where he worked, but this was to be especially distasteful.

The pump was installed in the center of the sump and could only be reached by crawling across a two-inch thick by eight-inch wide plank laying above the water. Evan gathered all the tools and materials that he needed. He opened the main cut-off electrical knife switch, and tagged it out. Then he emptied his pockets so that nothing would accidently drop into the sump. He crawled across the plank holding a drop-light, while the overly-large insects scurried to the ends of the wood, and its underside.

He wanted to make quick work of this job, and proceeded to loosen the packing gland, then used a packing puller to remove the old rings in the stuffing box. He used his eight-inch folding knife to cut and shape the new Teflon packing from its roll.

He wrapped each piece around the pump shaft, alternating the angled cuts, pushed the packing into the box, adjusted the steel gland holding the packing, then crawled back across the plank to start the pump, crawling back again to check for and adjust for proper, adequate, controlled leakage.

Despite the distraction of the difficulty of making this repair, there just wasn't any other way that Evan could have completed this project other than with thorough, best mechanical practice.

Another unpleasant, repeated task was the need each week to add five gallons of lubricating oil to the massive open tank of water, about the size of a typical backyard in-ground pool, installed in the engine room. The tank served as the reservoir for the pumps that moved the bank of hydraulically-operated passenger elevators, and the one freight elevator.

These elevators required this lubricated medium to operate the telephone-pole thick pistons that pushed the cars up through the nine stories of the building. When the elevators were called to lower floors, the liquid in the cylinders was returned to the water tank through valves.

The archaic method of adding oil to the tank, unchanged in more than sixty years, was to fill a bucket with the proper oil, then hand-carry it up an eight-foot high ladder and empty it into the open tank. It was hazardously slippery, and dark where the approach point to the tank was most accessible.

Although Evan had suggested that perhaps they could purchase a small hand-pump, then could rig a hose, or tubing, to transfer the oil from the bucket to the tank, it was the near-retirement aged Chief Engineer who did not see the need to change this obsolete process.

Apparently, that's the way it had always been done, and that's the way it was going to continue. Industrial Archeology 101.

In spite of the technical challenges, Evan continued to focus on performing his work to the best and most correct manner required. His integrity in carrying out his responsibilities, and his concern for this classic equipment was unshakeable.

During the next year on this job, it was fortunate that Evan met a like-minded soul. A friend of his had arranged a date with Abby, a woman about his age, who worked as an AutoCAD operator, that is, developing computer-aided design drawings, drafting plans for an architectural firm.

One of the firm's clients was a developer involved in renovating older structures in derelict sections of the City.

Evan and Abby immediately spoke the same language once they met. His archeological explorations in the deep recesses of his industrial setting complemented Abbey's field surveys of commercial and residential properties, in interpreting the vision of restoration builders. They started dating steadily, and during the next year, they blended into a committed relationship

In addition to their hands-on rescue of in-situ materials, their individual relationship histories included their previous marriages. Abby had been divorced following nine years in a disappointing marriage.

The archeological nature of their work-lives was well-suited to a caring partnership, and they were able to salvage their challenges to move forward together. He thought that here was an example of revitalizing history into a living, positive subject. His now long-ago depth of loneliness and despair had been replaced through a positive, vibrant relationship. With Abby's new-found confidence in finding positive affirmations in her life, their partnership was solidified and the excavation to find it was completed.

Eviction

Michael Hardisty was in the third year of his employment as a drafter and field technician at an architectural design and engineering consulting firm in New York City. In addition to architecture and consulting, the company stocked specialty mechanical equipment, such as steam pressure reducing valves, in their ground-floor storefront office, making these items immediately available to contractors on job sites.

The office entrance was accessed through the lobby of an apartment building owned by the firm's principal, Robert Shultz. This retail configuration provided contractors with the ability to pick up materials from the showroom and load them directly onto their vehicles, without the use of a loading dock. Besides this building, Robert owned several other residential and commercial properties in the city. He and his wife were completely financially independent.

Michael's responsibilities at the firm included translating preliminary architectural and engineering sketches developed by Robert following meetings with clients, into more formal drawings for review by him.

The shop consisted of Michael, Robert, and the office administrator and technical advisor, Marilyn Steward.

These projects involved moderate renovation work rather than the construction of new buildings. Establishing the drawings, and writing the specifications, were within Michael's province, with assistance by Marilyn. They had each been in the design industry for several years prior to joining Robert's shop.

In concert with Robert, they would utilize the services of selected consultants in various disciplines as required, in support of a project. Then, these basic sets of documents were presented to the clients for further review and comment, to finalize them into bid packages, to seek pricing by contractors.

As a small shop, Robert would limit the work load to what he thought the three of them could handle. His interest in these jobs was not exclusively for the money, although the fees, and the sale of equipment, derived a healthy income.

While Robert was certainly not opposed to making money, his focus in this enterprise was to win. His other business interests in real estate provided substantial compensation for his efforts.

His reputation as a knowledgeable and competent leader in the consulting community sustained his satisfaction, with his income secured by the residual aspects of collecting rent on his properties.

Michael's talent in visualizing the end products of sketches and notes from Robert and from participating in these conferences as well, to create meaningful drawings with specifications, was a great asset to the firm. With Marilyn's input as a proficient associate, it was a good team, ever mindful that Robert was the supreme boss.

In addition to the design elements of Michael's position, he was sometimes called upon to carry out other business functions for Robert. For example, he had been directed to appear at an Examinations Before Trial (EBT) in response to pending litigation regarding discrepancies in the payments from an estate for selected materials purchased from the firm. The case turned on the detail of an undecipherable set of items on an invoice.

Several times Michael had also been required to provide testimony at hearings before Administrative Law Judges.

These hearings were in response to building code violations for projects that Robert, as a Registered Architect and a registered Professional Engineer, had signed-off on.

Michael took his instructions from Robert in the manner and particulars of defending the firm's position, along with his own knowledge, and certainly contained his testimony to remain within the law. The firm did not often lose these cases which Robert expected.

And then there was the sub-team of Michael and Marilyn. She had been working for Robert for two years before Michael had hired on.

Now, during these several years while they were together, their role as colleagues and co-workers had moved beyond that to a full and satisfying relationship as friends and lovers. Both in their mid-forties, their affinity for detail, beauty, and customer service, along with their delight in the theatre, museums, and literature had sparked their romance.

Robert had not discouraged their liaison in the least and had encouraged their relationship. As demanding as he was in his businesses, he was nonetheless mindful of keeping these two staff members happy.

In deference to their employment, while they were united in their loyalty towards Robert, they were also similarly worn out by his insistence on prevailing against all adversaries.

Although this attitude of his was intrinsically understood by them, it prevented his compassion to be shown in many human situations, even though he had not presented this deficiency directly to them.

For example, there was the time when a superintendent at one of his buildings could not account for the excessive amount of cleaning supplies used over a period of several months.

To Robert, it was unquestionably the situation that this was the fault of the superintendent's pilfering activities rather than if it would have been based on other janitorial factors.

The consideration of tenant irresponsibility, or weather conditions for creating the need to use more supplies were not options. There was very little investigation. Robert terminated the employee.

And within Marilyn's set of tasks, besides supervising the professional office and showroom, was her responsibility to manage Robert's rent rolls. Tenants checks were mailed to the office for processing and banking by Marilyn.

She maintained the long lists of renters and the properties associated with their accounts, by hand – this time period in their business was still only on the edge of computerization. Robert had not upgraded to a more modern electronic method of record-keeping, nor to the emerging technology of computer-aided design.

Sometimes, tenants were late with their payments. As a property owner, Robert had specific lease terms in place, in conformance with standard business practices. This did not leave room for the human element.

On more than one occasion, following all prescribed procedures and certified notices, Michael and Marilyn, as the owner's representatives, had been assigned the duty of witnessing the eviction of a residential tenant.

These evictions were carried out by a City Marshall engaged through legal means and utilizing any number of moving companies that had been contracted by the City to execute the procedure.

While Michael and Marilyn were certainly business-minded, and understood the necessity for these actions, it was heartbreaking for them to participate.

The movers exercised a level of care to limit damages while packing things away, however, watching other people's personal effects being indiscriminately thrust into impersonal boxes was extremely sad.

Following the third exercise in this ruthless, but necessary display of business management and social anguish, Michael and Marilyn knew that they could not keep doing this, and could not continue to have a positive emotional feeling towards Robert.

Nonetheless, they certainly wanted to keep their jobs serving the needs of their clients, contractors, and their boss. Would this be a simple matter of expressing their feelings to Robert? They would just have to find this out, perhaps with a logical suggestion that Robert could find someone else to represent his interests in these proceedings.

They approached him one day with this simple solution to contract out. His reaction was not what they had feared. He looked at them and agreed that if their hearts were not in it, then it couldn't work. From that point on, Robert found a family member of his, a certified para-legal who would take care of this unpleasantness, and the matter was closed.

Thankful for not being evicted from their jobs, Michael and Marilyn went back to company work and continued their relationship, now not distracted by side-jobs.

Happy Anniversary

It was the eighth anniversary of Philip's divorce. He and Brenda had also celebrated their eighth wedding anniversary those many years ago, when the marriage had disintegrated. Philip and Brenda had been happy together, for most of the first years of their marriage.

With the coming of Brenda's dissatisfaction of her career plans in the field of media production, Philip maintained his isolation in the comfort of his satisfying work life as a photographer. It was difficult for Philip to concentrate on Brenda's turmoil when he was untroubled by his occupational envelope.

For Philip, he felt like the years since the end of their marriage had been filled with thin slices of days darkening to a shade of obscurity, punctuated by moments of lucid deliberation, in deference to a paraphrased passage written by the author John Updike. Until he met Celeste, also divorced, when a bright future was revealed.

Now, for Philip, and for his new bride to be, their awakening from the misery of loneliness was a shout to the broadest reaches of human emotions.

Once each of the former marriages had been over for Philip and Celeste, their individual time alone was spent in reflection, anger, and the wistful grasp of memorializing what could have been.

The next few years on their own, before they met each other, were taken up with attempts to connect with new interests, and new relationships, but the wall of hurt and searching took its toll.

While Philip had been struggling along the deepest valley of regret for his part of the blame for his and Brenda's collapse, Celeste, divorced for six years, had been suffocating within her cave of despair created by the loss of her husband, Tremaine.

For Celeste, following ten years of seemingly wedded bliss, there was no hint of Tremaine's dalliance in his involvement with a new partner. Their demise as a couple came relatively swiftly as Tremaine drifted away in his new relationship, until Celeste was completely abandoned, and the marriage needed to end.

For Philip and Brenda, the split took a little longer, but not by much. Receiving almost no sympathy because of Philip's attitude of callous ignorance, Brenda did not find a reason to stay in their union.

After losing Brenda, Philip would have encounters with prospective partners, where he mumbled through an evening of stilted, halting, conversation. Or, he missed the opportunity to connect with someone while the distraction of thinking about Brenda created an almost catatonic state.

It was during this transition from being in a committed relationship when, after some time in the abyss of divorce, he began the slow climb into the refreshing state of realizing that his obvious emotional and empathetic shortcomings had destroyed his marriage.

He was, then, wiser, and on the mend towards a new, meaningful, and hoped-for successful peace with a new partner.

For Celeste, after Tremaine was gone, she had tentatively stepped out on arranged dates, or to other group events, but she was hurt, unsure of her worth, and missed out on the potential for relief by her own inaccurately perceived fault in losing Tremaine.

After a few years of these hesitations, and wasted opportunities, she too progressed to the understanding that her actions were not to be blamed for the disappearance of Tremaine, and that she might now find renewed happiness.

It was a hard stretch of years for each of them, until Philip and Celeste converged. Philip had an assignment to photograph a sixtieth wedding anniversary for a couple with a large family. Celeste, a long-time and accomplished chef, as well as a business professional, was managing the catering side of the restaurant where the party was being held.

In their respective roles as photographer, and host, it was imperative that they coordinate, and cooperate on the serving schedule, decorations, and timing. And this day of congregating seemed to be fashioned for their time together as well.

They had talked briefly on the phone when Philip was booked for the job, then he showed up in person.

Throughout the day, with Philip taking a series of standardized set-up photos, and other candid pictures in order to put the event's album together, with Celeste directing traffic for table service, and guiding the highlighted parts of the festivities, it did not take very long for their interest in each other to be recognized.

At the close of the affair, Philip was bold enough to ask Celeste if she might want to step out of her catering functions to be served at another restaurant for dinner. Celeste was confident enough to say yes.

Their first evening together demonstrated reserved emotions, but their conversational exchanges were fruitful. They scheduled another date, then another, and continued to get to know each other.

And, following the next two years of forgiving, and loving, with their former challenges ever-present, but fading, they were prepared to accept what they realized to be true, that there were new joys to be shared.

Hymn 693

Just as I am, without one plea,
But that Thy blood was shed for me,
And that Thou bid'st me come to Thee,
O Lamb of God, I come.

That's how this haunting hymn starts from the Protestant Episcopal Church Hymnal.

Just how Stuart was a few years before hearing that one, before understanding its power, that's what he was thinking of as the tears came down his face while the organ music came up to introduce this one. He could never get through not even the first line of this hymn without starting to cry. It had been that way since he had first heard this one, and ever since then leading up to, and following choosing this hymn and others for inclusion in his adult Baptism.

The hymn goes on, in some of the following stanzas,

Just as I am, Thou wilt receive,
Wilt welcome, pardon, cleanse, relieve;
Because Thy promise I believe,
O Lamb of God, I come.

Standing next to his wife Melissa of the past thirty-five years, he couldn't look at her – he didn't have to. He knew that she knew he was crying. It wasn't fair when this hymn was chosen for the church service without Stuart knowing it was coming beforehand – he was always affected by it.

Just as he was more than forty years before, now standing there in this pew in this church, barely able to form the words to follow this hymn, when he had not known the hymns. He had not been raised as an Episcopalian, nor even within any other Protestant denomination, or in any other form of organized religion. His childhood and youth were not filled with spirit, unless one would call the misery of meanness spirit.

Melissa turned to him and gently placed her hand over his as he was holding the book, while she continued to sing, softly.

He moved just a half-step closer to her, touching her thigh with his. She held her hand there, understanding.

His journey as a Christian had not been startling, but slow and complicated. First, as a child believing in nothing - that would only lead to desolation, and then learning to understand that the wretchedness of his youth days could be the foundation for his salvation.

He was only eight when he had to act as the parent to his drunken father. With his mother having died when Stuart was six, his dad would drink almost a half-quart of rye whiskey every single day at his job on the crew of ironworkers traveling to various city parks to restore wrought-iron or chain-link fencing.

It seemed so easy for his father to drink like that, relying on his apparently undiminished skill to line up fence sections, and to stretch chain-link to attach to uprights. As Stuart had met the members of the ironworker gang during the department's Christmas parties, he could see that they had special ways of covering for each other's vices, which included drinking, playing the numbers, and completing as much work as was deemed sufficiently adequate to meet established standards.

Things were a little different back in the 1960s when his father worked with this crew and as Stuart was growing up.

At first, Stuart had not been thinking about drinking, not at eight years old, but then, when he was eleven and in the sixth grade, his journey began with a group of his classmates at the new school that he was now attending. The family, that is, his father and one sister, Patty, just three years older than Stuart, had moved to another neighborhood, just across the boundary line that forced his enrollment in a new elementary school for this final grade.

Meeting the new group on that first day of school, it didn't take but just that first weekend when he was invited to join them at one of their houses, where they could kick-off the weekend by opening fresh packs of cigarettes, and fresh bottles of Night Train, Bali Hi, Ripple, or Thunderbird, four of the cheapest wines on the market.

It was one of the boys in the group, also aged about eleven or twelve, who had an older brother of eighteen who would buy cigarettes and wine for the others. Smoking cigarettes, and choking to acclimate himself to them, was not as easy as taking that first slug of wine. Drinking became no challenge at all, and Stuart adapted himself to it quite easily.

From then on, as the weekends passed, he increasingly needed more alcohol and each successive weekend became a blur of scrambling for wine, with the occasional purchase of Four Roses, a relatively inexpensive rye whiskey.

The boys would be in the alleys between apartment buildings, or in someone's house if no adults were home, where they would smoke, drink, and engage in various heavy petting games with some of their female classmates, like one called "Truth, Dare, Consequences, Promise or Repeat." Relatively tame, but nonetheless risqué enough for elementary and middle school students.

Stuart would walk home, unsteadily, but once in the door and meeting his father, who was already in his own stage of drunkenness, who didn't notice and didn't pay attention to his son's condition, Stuart was not under any scrutiny. Stuart's sister, at fourteen, was already out of the house with her friends most of the time after school and on the weekends and didn't have Stuart on her mind either.

Throughout his sixth-grade year, Stuart would follow this habitual pattern of drinking and socializing. Carrying this forward during the seventh through ninth grades of junior high school did not become as debilitating as it could have been, as Stuart did not have a lot of money to spend on alcohol.

He would somehow manage, however, with his bicycle newspaper route money.

Many boys, not girls at the time, had paper routes and Stuart could earn enough money to find someone who would be willing to purchase wine or whiskey for him.

Cigarettes were less expensive in those days and cashing in empty soda bottles for their deposit money, with some supplemental paper route money usually resulted in the ability to purchase cigarettes.

Once in high school, he was able to hire on in one of the local candy stores in the neighborhood, cleaning the floors, stocking shelves, and occasionally, serving customers. He was earning more money than what he had been generating from his paper route, and he was able to secure alcohol on a regular basis.

As he then turned sixteen beginning his last two years in high school, he was able to secure a position in food service at a neighborhood grocery store. Working after school, and on alternating weekends, checking in deliveries, stocking shelves, collecting trash and helping to carry groceries to customers cars, provided even more pay, making his alcohol purchases somewhat more accessible.

When he turned eighteen as he graduated high school, since the drinking age was still that age in the late 1960s, he could now buy his own liquor.

Now, as a high school graduate, and having taken various shop courses, he was successful in being hired as a helper in a carpentry shop, joined the union local, and was on a track for a formal apprenticeship program. Earning more money, however, only made it more comfortable to stay plied with alcohol. He would be drinking most anything, but his preference was beer.

His career path, or at least job progress, was interrupted briefly by an obligatory two-year stint in the Army. He was able to sustain his drinking habit once he had finished basic training by serving in a relatively stable daily work environment in building maintenance and being promoted to Corporal.

Unless he had the duty on the occasional rotating weekend schedule, he was free after work during the week and for most weekends. He was able to leave the State-side base where he was stationed, joining with other soldiers to spend time at bars and other social enterprises.

Following the Army, he returned to his boyhood city, and with his mechanical training, secured a job at a college campus as a maintenance mechanic.

His responsibilities included walking throughout the campus from building to building wearing a tool belt, and responding to work tickets distributed to the mechanics each morning by the maintenance supervisor.

During the first few weeks on the job, he was paired with a more senior mechanic who was able to show Stuart around the campus to the various buildings where repair jobs were waiting to be completed. After several weeks, unless a job required more than one mechanic, he would be assigned to work alone.

His level of drinking and access to alcohol was not overly affected by this environment. Soon after starting work there, he was able to identify a dozen places where he could hide single pint flasks of whisky in various crevices of basement walls, in between piping runs, and in rarely occupied offices. He had been provided with a set of keys to all spaces and cabinets. It was extremely convenient for him to be working there.

From long practice in drinking and working, he was able to maintain his equilibrium throughout the day while nipping at his stock.

But he wasn't satisfied. At the end of the day in the early afternoon he would clock out, then walk to his car in the parking lot.

Two blocks down the street at the corner was a grocery store. He stopped his car and went into the place to purchase a six-pack of beer for the ride home, which he could finish at least two of the cans before finding a parking place near his apartment building.

The rest of the evening included more drinking, watching television, and sometimes, if he wasn't too tired, going to a local bar to meet several friends. After just a year of this life, it did become boring. Without really thinking about it, or even looking around for it, he did meet a woman in one of the college administrative departments who was friendly to him and he reciprocated.

There in Melissa's office to install a thermostatic radiator valve to control the heat near her desk, she started a conversation by asking what he was doing and how long he had been working there.

With his morning alcohol content making him shine, he was clever in his responses and by the time he had completed the work, they arranged to go out at the end of the week.

Their first date started at a restaurant and included several cocktails. Melissa drank, but apparently, she was not an alcoholic. Stuart bested her at the meal by consuming double the number of drinks that Melissa had ordered.

At the time, it didn't seem to Stuart that she noticed or minded his drinking on this date and then on subsequent dates. Stuart maintained his equilibrium and charm. Melissa was a kind, friendly and helpful person. Working at the college together, seeing each other regularly and sharing in a similar demeanor, their friendship and romance advanced into full-bloom love.

After a few months of being together, meeting each other's families and willing to open-up to each other, Melissa suggested that they attend a service at her church.

Now, of course, Stuart had not been raised in the church, but his feelings for Melissa led him to be compelled to join her one Sunday morning. A typical Episcopal service, there was an opening hymn, a reading from the Old Testament, the congregational shared reading of a transitional Psalm, a reading from the New Testament, the reading of the appointed Gospel passage, and then the Sermon.

Stuart was only mildly focused. He gladly took the tiny sip of wine for Communion, but he had already come to the church with a half-quart bottle of wine in his system. Melissa was none the wiser. She was serene in her having Stuart at her side in her church family, looking to have Stuart embrace this life with her.

During the next year, they continued their relationship, they shared in church services, but for Stuart, not on every Sunday.

Most Sundays would leave him facing the ravages of the Saturday nights filled with drinking and not eating. He was adept at managing to keep his drunkenness separate from his time with Melissa.

And so, in spite of even how thinly veiled from Melissa this part of his existence was, she was unwavering in her love for him.

They rented an apartment together and were married in the church. Their life together now involved Stuart's cleverness in maintaining hidden stashes of alcohol in special places around the apartment, in his car, back at the college work-place and sustaining his responsibilities in keeping his job and keeping Melissa happy.

Two years after their wedding, they bought a house and had their first child, a daughter, Mary. Two years later, a son, Ben. The children were baptized, their life continued with Stuart attending church intermittently, until the children were old enough for Sunday school. Even then, Stuart did not change his habitual drinking and continued skipping church services.

While Melissa was outwardly tolerant, she began the slow slide away from accepting Stuart's total immersion in his alcohol abuse. She started to distance herself from standing together with him in ignoring the obvious – that this just couldn't go on in the same way.

The first major event in the tearing away of the envelope of complacency came the night before they had planned to shop for a new pair of shoes for Mary. That night, with the children asleep, Melissa looked in the kitchen drawer where they kept several hundred dollars of ready money saved over several weeks for groceries, gas, and shoes. Nothing there.

Melissa was besides herself. *Did Stuart drink all of it away? What did he do with it?*

Stepping away from her calmness, she screamed at him in the living room, "Stuart! Where is Mary's shoe money! What did you do with it?"

Sitting, staring at the television set, Stuart jerked his head up. "What are you talking about?" he called back

Melissa stomped in. "I'm talking about the money that's supposed to be where it's supposed to be in the kitchen drawer. That was money for Mary's shoes which we need to get tomorrow. What is the matter with you? Where is that money!" Melissa's intervening years of quiet and ignoring Stuart's inescapable irresponsibility were over the edge of her acquiescence.

"I'll find it," he said.

"How do I know it's here in this house and you didn't swallow it away?" she said.

"As much of a drunk as I am, even I couldn't drink away that much cash in so short a time," he said.

"Well, just find it."

He squeezed his brain to think. He started looking in some of his bottle hiding places. Some of the easy ones – the hamper in their bathroom; under the stairs leading to the basement; behind the furnace down there; in the enclosure for the trash cans at the side of the house; in a junked cabinet in the garage.

Walking back into the kitchen and fortified with two shots of rye whisky from one of the hidden bottles, he stared at the refrigerator. A dim vision began to reveal itself. Almost without thought, trance-like, he opened the freezer door. There in a plastic bag in among the hamburger meat – the wad of money. For what reason he had placed it there from the kitchen drawer was beyond his comprehension.

He walked into their bedroom. Melissa was sitting on the edge of her side of the bed. He didn't say anything, just handed her the bag. She said not a word. She placed the bag in her night-table drawer, climbed under the covers, and shut out the light.

Stuart said not a word and did the same.

They shopped for Mary's shoes the next day, barely speaking. Time would move on and Melissa never mentioned it again.

The second major event that would stop Stuart almost cold from his life-long alcohol dependence came just a few months later. It was a Friday night. Stuart got off work and went directly to one of the bars in their neighborhood.

Melissa went directly home to meet the children after school. She didn't expect to see Stuart until much later in the evening, this being the start of another distracted, drink-filled weekend.

Stuart had several beers, then he had a few more. It was getting on to 11:30 p.m. and time for him to go home. He left the bar, fumbled for the keys to his car, opened the door, and sat behind the wheel. *Yeah, I'm fine to drive home.*

He started the car and slowly pulled out of the parking lot into the road. He turned on the radio and weaved towards the first intersection. He didn't see the light turn red and went straight through the intersection. He didn't see the pedestrian in the crosswalk until he almost brushed him with the passenger side of the car. He stopped at the next corner, looking back in his mirror. The pedestrian had disappeared.

This did it for Stuart. An explosion of an Epiphany. The life of that person crossing the street and his own life would have ended in a finality that could never be recaptured, unless in Heaven. God had spared them this night and Stuart's drinking life was over, so he vowed.

He called Melissa from his cell phone. "Honey, I've had it. I've taken my last drink. Please come down to one block before the Blue Moon. It's over, I'm getting sober. Please come soon sweetheart, I'm ready to come home."

Melissa drove to his car, now parked against the curb. He got in to hers and they drove to the house.

The next morning, Saturday, Stuart resisted getting a drink from any one of his many stashes. Instead, he went around the house and retrieved almost all the hidden bottles and poured their contents down the drain. Almost all. He knew that while he had made a solemn promise that this was the end, he just couldn't quite face the reality of making that hard and fast commitment. He bargained with himself that instead of cold turkey he could ease himself away from the drink.

The next few weeks were a mix of sipping alcohol while struggling with the shame of not stopping. He did not speak of any of this with Melissa. He sensed that she was on the edge of seeing his breaking through, but she wasn't speaking about it, and he couldn't open-up to her.

Reaching near to the end of his last stashed bottle, he made the final resolve not to purchase another. Then he called a friend of his who had joined a twelve-step program and had always urged Stuart to join him in the struggle to get sober and stay that way.

The friend drove over to Stuart's house and spent the next few hours talking about what Stuart had to face and what could be the outcome if he gave himself to the program and the effort it would take to change his life.

During the next several months Stuart began attending Alcoholics Anonymous meetings in his awakening commitment to recovery. He began to attend church regularly on Sundays, to the delight and relief of Melissa and the children. He made it a point now to follow the service, to comprehend it and to listen to the hymns. That's when he discovered the sections on Christian Responsibility, and Christian Life. These entire sections focused on being humble, and in that regard not thinking less of oneself, but thinking of oneself less, by putting into action the works of Christianity. These hymns were a powerful backdrop to his awakening to spirituality.

The words and melody of Hymn 693 especially spoke to his journey through the bleakness of recovery to hope.

Stuart's new commitment to his family, his church and the world community led him within a year to his decision to be baptized as a Christian. Learning that baptism into the covenant of resisting wickedness, renouncing corruption and embracing forgiveness would lead to trusting in the grace of God provided the avenue for his peace. To the delight of Melissa, Mary, Ben and the congregation, he was baptized, crying throughout Hymn 693.

Connections

Author's Note:

This piece was written in response to a writer's group prompt that required the inclusion of several selected characters in various life situations. The exercise demanded some device of interconnecting their relationships. Creating a reunion seemed to be one way to accomplish this. The assignment included the following six characters in search of a story:

Grave digger (male)	-	*Anthony Spires*
Restaurateur (male)	-	*Franklin Sorte*
Disabled late teen (male)	-	*Robert Thompson*
Established lawyer, retired or near retirement-age (black female)	-	*Patricia Thompson*
Teacher (female)	-	*Katherine Muncie*
Sports-related career (female)	-	*Sharon Billings*

7/2/15 – 7/3/18

It was raining. Anthony Spires reached for the front door handle of the catering hall and stepped into the lobby.

"Welcome to our homecoming, and for some of you, a fortieth reunion," said a nicely-dressed woman sitting at a small table. Anthony did not recognize her. "Did you pre-register?" She continued, looking at a list.

"I did," Anthony answered. Before she asked the next question, he stated his name, which she found. She offered him a name tag which, in addition to identification, noted the college graduation year 1975.

"Please step into the hall," she said. "You'll find your table number, then please go in and make yourself comfortable." He couldn't make out her name, but it wasn't important. He wasn't here to see her.

Stepping into a foyer, he found his card and walked into a large room set up with dinner tables and additional chairs along the walls. Several people were sitting at different tables, and a few at the chairs. Most were holding drinks. He stepped up to the bar near the entrance and ordered a gin and tonic.

He found his table and placed his card and drink where he wanted to sit. No one was there.

He walked to a small group at the side chairs. He lifted his hand in acknowledgement, but he only recognized one person.

He did not have to look at her tag to see that it was Patricia Thompson. She stood as he approached.

"Anthony, how are you?" she asked softly.

"I'm good, Patricia," he said. "It's been so long. I wasn't sure that you would be joining us, you being so busy and all."

"Well, I really didn't want to miss this one since we almost never see each other."

"Almost? I'm sure you just mean never. Besides a view on Facebook, we haven't been together more than once since back in the day after graduation."

"Well, yes, I guess that is what I mean. And how did you figure out that I was busy?"

"Because I remembered that you were driven to go into the law, and knowing you, I wasn't surprised that's how it went. I did see your name on Facebook once, but I don't know how it works, so I never really "friended you" as they say to keep in touch. I saw that you were an attorney, and that's how it seemed to me that you must be busy."

"You're right," she said. "I was going to pursue my law degree after graduation, and I did. First, I did a Masters' Program in Political Science at Northwestern, then I was accepted to Georgetown in Washington, DC. After I got my JD, I started as a Law Clerk in a medium-sized firm and stayed there for a few years. Then I got a spot as a Deputy Defense Attorney in a County office for the next few years until I opened my own practice. I am busy, that's for sure, but like I said I wanted to be here tonight and was hoping to see you. I don't use Facebook either, so I wouldn't have followed along with you anyway."

"Yeah, Facebook is just a mystery to us oldsters," he said. "Not something that was invented when we were coming up. But you being a defender and in your own practice – that must have been a tough road for a black woman, I'm sure."

"It had its moments," she said. "But I plowed right through that nonsense and made it happen. Now, I'm almost done with it and heading into retirement."

"Yes, we're all getting there at our age," Anthony said. "But one of the things that I really admired about you when we were young and going together was that you were so direct and not afraid of anything."

"I was much too shy and not too brave," he said.

"Anthony," she said, "during school I leaned on you as this quiet, but confident white guy who was willing to pair up with this young, but feisty sister. Believe me, I felt safe and cared for when I was with you. I thought we were going places together, and then we graduated."

"I know," he said. "It was this wonderful, dreamy time when we were taking Social Psychology, Anthropology, and Art History, and then we would go back to my apartment to study for a while before we couldn't stand it anymore and would jump into that big Queen-sized bed of mine to take care of our needs."

"Well, aren't you the clinical one, my friend? But, yes, indeed, we sure had the hots for each other then," she said. "I would tell my parents that we were studying for an exam. I had no doubt that they knew we were fooling around, but they liked you, and we were adults and it could be that way."

"Adults?" he asked. "Maybe on the edge of that, but we had a time to go to get there. Even for me, then, just out of the Army and back from Vietnam, I had to struggle with demons and courage and planning for the future."

"That's funny," she said. "I thought you were so strong, this gentle giant, and didn't see you struggling. You seemed pretty adjusted and didn't talk much about the Army or the war. If anything, it was me who had the struggles, knowing where I was going, but trying to figure out how to get there, and then what was I going to do about you? I knew that we were right for each other, or at least, right for me - it was the world that wasn't right for us."

"I know what you mean," Anthony said. "I was happy being with you and loving you. I wasn't overly troubled by my service time. I wasn't even thinking much about keeping us going. It was obvious that the rest of the people in our little corner of the world, even as enlightened as they were in, wow, the early-seventies, weren't always nice to us walking around together, especially when we held hands or kissed in public. We talked about it, sometimes, but it didn't seem to matter much. We were young and in love."

"Well, maybe you didn't talk about it much, but I remember mentioning it more than a few times," Patricia said. "After all, you would be taking me home to my mostly black neighborhood, and we had to face those looks of, well, those looks, even in the 'Renaissance' of the seventies."

"It sure wasn't comfortable then. But I had you."

"I don't know," he said. "I didn't pay much attention to it — I was more idealistic than you. I believed. I was oblivious. You weren't fooled because you are a bright and sensitive person. I guess our relationship just couldn't sustain itself once we were out of school when we had been in this envelope. When we were there, we had this entourage of supporters. Remember Katherine Muncie? She was really a good friend of ours. I knew that she was going into teaching, so I wonder how she made out? I guess she must be retiring also. And Franklin Sorte? He was on our side, too. I know he always liked to cook and to talk about food. I wonder if he ever opened that restaurant he was thinking about."

"Right," Patricia said. "We had Sharon Billings, too. She was so wonderful and friendly. She was good in sports and played on the women's basketball team. I know she said that she didn't think she could get anywhere in sports — I don't think they had the WNBA back then, but she thought maybe she'd be going into sports management or sporting goods sales. I don't know how she did. Maybe we'll see them tonight. But never mind them, how about you, Anthony? What happened to you?"

"Oh, I had my liberal arts degree, but I was still loose about what I was going to do with it. I was going to school under the GI Bill, and didn't think much about the next step after graduation. I needed money, and since I operated construction equipment in the Army, I found a job with a cemetery monument company where I was resetting headstones and digging graves."

"Oh my," Patricia said. "That seems kind of spooky."

"Not really. After all, we didn't do these things at night, which really would have been weird, but it was more of a service to others and I stayed with the company until I retired just this past year at union scale. I didn't have to hand-dig graves since I operated the back hoe, but I had to be around funerals and burials, and then filled-in the graves when they were done."

"Straightening headstones also worked for me, reading the epitaphs and helping to keep these cemeteries well-ordered and nice. The families appreciated this perpetual care, I'm sure. I didn't use my degree much, but was happy in my work, and volunteered with different community groups and youth organizations. But what about you, Patricia? Besides the law, what else is going on?"

"Well, like I said, after a few years I did open my own practice, with two partners. We were mostly litigating civil cases, so there was less of an emotional attachment than when I was serving in the District Attorney's office, but it was a slice."

"I got married about ten years after school to a very nice black man who owns a structural engineering consulting firm, and we have two children. My daughter Alicia is a social worker and my son Robert is nineteen and in college right now studying architecture, but he's disabled. He was born with one leg shorter than the other and uses a brace, but he's a brave lad and nothing stops him."

"That's impressive about your husband and children. Too bad about Robert, but it sounds positive and seems like a nice life."

"Things are good," she said. But what about you, Anthony? What's been happening in your family life?"

"Well, I met someone soon after college, my wife Jennifer now of almost forty years. She's a manager with a retail gardening supplier, and we have three children, Tom, a house painter with a commercial firm, Betsy who writes a column for a national magazine, and Lillian who is wrapping up college, majoring in digital photography and fashion design."

"We're doing fine. I always do miss those long-ago college days of hope and being spontaneous, though."

"Me too," Patricia said. "It was a time in our lives when we could be casual, yet we needed to be serious, too. I know I took our relationship seriously, and I miss those times."

"Of course. Too bad we needed to move on from there," Anthony said. "Those were great days of promise, and great music. But it basically seems to have worked out."

"It sounds like we didn't have bad lives. It's just that we lost what you and I had personally, but that's how it is sometimes. Now we move on again, after tonight"

"I know," she said. "We had something then, and now we just have this reunion. It'll just have to do. I'd like to still hold on to these things, but it'll just have to be the reflections of days past. Wait, isn't that a Moody Blues number?" she continued.

"It is, almost," he said. "It's an album called *Days of Future Past.*' It's like the quote I always use, 'Today will be yesterday, tomorrow.' Makes sense to me but not everyone gets it."

"I get it," she said. "And, we can't go home again either, there's another one."

"That's for sure," he said. "But we will be going home after this evening, so if I don't see you later in the crowd after the speeches, please take care of yourself."

"I will. It was good to see you, Anthony. Brought back some fond memories."

"It did for me, too, Patricia. Something I can hold on to with real affection."

They exchanged a brief kiss, and as the hall was now filling up, they parted to their respective tables. Following dinner and presentations, Anthony left the room, walked into the foyer and out to the street. It was still raining.

Snippets

Four Before One

Does R22 refrigerant boil at 54° Fahrenheit? Adding 22° to 0° Centigrade, which is 32° Fahrenheit, gets you to the number 54. I wonder if R22 refrigerant is called that number to match its boiling point? Or maybe it's related to its cosmic weight? That answer will have to wait until I can look it up.

I used to have all kinds of numbers ready. The volume of a cubic foot of water (8.33 gallons, in case you wanted to know). The boiling point of water (212° but only at sea level). The speed of light — 186,000 miles per second.

I can't keep those facts handy now, these days, after Cynthia left. Back then, it had been me, and Cynthia, and Janey, and Tom. We had been the four of us. A family. Not that there aren't lots of other numbers in families. To be a family, two is the minimum. One does not make a family. One is just one person. I thought all four of us were happy in this family.

Apparently, though only three of us were happy. Me, and Janey, and Tom. Cynthia must have been happy, for a while anyway. Then, like pale slices of days darkening to a fatal shade, as John Updike writes, happiness was blocked, and it slipped away.

Together with Cynthia for fifteen years, the children approaching pre-teen years, then, gone.

I didn't light her fire anymore – she walked away, and took the children with her. It had been just the two of us at first, Cynthia and me. We were happy. Cynthia seemed happy. I was happy, at least. I didn't see the break-up coming. I just stumbled through the relationship, played with the children, went to work, brought her presents for her birthday, for Christmas, listened to her when she talked.

I guess she couldn't help it – I was just too quiet. But sometimes I spoke up. Like the time that I said no, she couldn't go to the movies that night with a friend of hers. She hadn't put supper on the table yet, the children's clothes needed washing. Why would I have let her out? Things needed attention.

You can't have someone just do what they want – there were things that had to get done, not only on that night, but at other times too. How about when she wanted me to drop the children off at school, even though she was going out as well for a doctor's appointment? Why couldn't she take care of taking them to school on her way?

After all, I had to meet Jackson to go to the track. We needed to make the first race at 1:00 pm. I couldn't be late to meet Jackson, so she had to take the children to school on her way to the doctor. This was just the way it was.

Time to Leave

Hilton stood facing Vera in front of her house.

"I can't take you looking at every tomato that passes by," she said.

"I don't do that."

"You look every time."

"Now you look," he said. "That's what men do. But I'm still all for you."

"Every man I've been with looked, but you touched someone else. I'm not letting this go."

"You think I did something with someone else? You thinking that won't stop me from looking."

"You won't be looking and you won't be touching me again."

"Honey, don't you know that I'm the only man for you."

"What I know is that the only man you are is stupid. You are a no-account misery of an excuse for a man."

"Well, then, I guess this is my time to leave and my time to find someone else," he said.

"You're right about that. If you think you can find someone. There's no woman who will give you the time of day."

"That's what I like about you, you lay it right out there," he said.

"You like that? You have more feelings than I thought."

"Sweetheart, I don't care what you believe about me touching someone else – I've only got fingers for you. I swear on everything righteous I will stop the roving eyes. Would that do it?"

"I don't know."

"Just give me some time to prove myself."

"Alright, I'll try."

"That's good. You won't be sorry."

"We'll see," she said.

Blizzard Flower

It had snowed heavily that day. More than he had seen it in any one day since three years ago, when Grayson had moved the family to that small cabin in Watertown, New York on the edge of Lake Ontario.

His wife Janey, and their eight and ten-year old daughters Sharon and Rachel, were not excited about moving from the relative warmth of Binghamton, near Pennsylvania, but their two older sons, Peter, fourteen and George, sixteen, were way more amused than the girls were apprehensive. It didn't seem to matter to the male counterparts of the family wherever they lived, but the females were definitely feeling the tugs of change.

Grayson had accepted a position as a supervisor of a production line at a tool manufacturing plant, his now third career move in the past ten years. Janey, as a State certified elementary school teacher, had been able to find a place in the school systems to which they had relocated, however, it was not hidden from anyone in the family that she had been worn out each time they moved. Their daughters had picked up on that, while Grayson and the boys had not shown much reaction, nor had they concealed their feelings very well.

Grayson never spoke about his feelings to Janey, and nor to anyone else.

If Sharon and Rachel had said anything, it must have been to their mother only, since Grayson had not heard them speak of it, or he just didn't hear it. Peter and George took after their father, and never said anything much at all, at least not that Grayson heard.

This was of little concern to Grayson. If things looked calm and quiet, then they were. There weren't many emotions or opinions that ever seemed to reach the surface of his intellect to blossom into conversation. Janey, and their daughters, when they did speak to him, always seemed to him like they weren't talking about anything important. Grayson never caught on to what Janey knew, that he was a fool.

It was time for school this morning. Despite the weather, it was on. The girls were off to grade school by bus, the boys by bus on their way to middle school, and the high school. Janey had the third grade, though Sharon was not in her class. Rachel, in sixth grade, also escaped toeing the mark in direct contact with her mother. The boys, usually quite self-sufficient, were doing just fine at their schools.

Janey was not doing well. Although she enjoyed her students while she delivered her carefully crafted lesson plans in language arts, math and science, once the day was over, she had to trudge back to her husband.

Her daughters' and her sons' loyalties did not make up enough for her to get over having to concentrate on pretending to listen to Grayson's monotone of complaints about his dead-end jobs, now in their third incarnation. It was draining the life out of her. It was destroying any show of beauty in her world.

There was only one hint of pretty – like a lone blade of grass remaining on a snow-covered hilltop, it was her plan to take the children away from the sustained, periodic destructive uprooting of their home life.

Did she think that wrestling the children away from their father, and she from her husband, would be a solution to the endless uncertainty of their missing continuity? Yes, she did.

Boating to Music

<u>*Author's Note:*</u>

The following play is included in this collection as an illustration of the technique of building a written piece using the specific requirements of including selected words or phrases. Composed in July 2013, this short play was created in concert (no pun intended) with the author's brief stint attending the local community's playwright's group. Displayed in standard play format as recommended by the group, it is completely frivolous, and simply an exercise in fun.

<u>*Required Words:*</u>

Nutrition
Technophobe
Foreign
Asafetida
Mandocello
Polynesian
Circuitous

CHARACTERS:

JUANITA:	A school teacher, age late thirties, dressed in business attire, holding a book
JASON:	A strong sailor, age late twenties, wearing a woolen watch cap; Captain of the boat
FRANKLIN:	A musician, age late sixties, scruffily dressed, holding a saxophone
ORIENTO:	A carpenter, age mid-thirties, dressed in coveralls, holding a saw, and a steel yardstick
DONATARI:	A worldly hustler, age mid-fifties, wearing a loud sports jacket, holding a deck of cards

SETTING:

A small, unadorned sailboat on open water containing four passengers seated at the gunwales and facing each other; another person at the stern holding the tiller; the sail does not block their view of each other; the weather is calm, the sun is shining; these are a group of people who appear to have been together for some time on this journey.

In the sailboat, daylight, four passengers and the captain; first character speaks.

JUANITA

(Looking up from her open book)

(Brightly) What do you think about today's weather? It says in my book that days like this can make people happy. I'm happy today.

JASON

(Holding the tiller with one hand)

(Friendly) I know I'm happy. I've got my little group of **foreign** people in this wooden boat. Well, you're all foreign to me anyway since I didn't know everyone very well when we started, and I like my wooden boat.

FRANKLIN

(Holding the saxophone at his side)

(Chiding) You would say that about a wooden boat, being the **technophobe** that you are. Look at you, Captain of a sailing vessel. Why aren't we in a motor launch? Because you wanted to take us slowly on this **circuitous** route, didn't you?

ORIENTO

(Holding the saw and yardstick on his lap)

(Abruptly) Now wait a minute. It's not his fault that we're in this pickle. I'm the one who built this scow. I'll admit it was me who wanted to re-plant ourselves in a **Polynesian** paradise, spreading our music throughout the land, but I wanted to add an instrument to our repertoire. I thought in a sailboat we'd make a big impression on strangers while we searched for that elusive **mandocello**.

DONATARI

(Fingering the deck of cards)

(Sarcastically) Yeah, what do you know about it? I'm the one who told everyone that we needed more **nutrition**, not just more music. That's why I suggested we not only sooth the savage beast with our musical compositions, but we provide little plates of cooked **asafetida** root wrapped in spinach leaves as enticements for our concerts. These morsels would help the music go down and would ward off evil spirits.

JUANITA

(Indignantly) Well, I wasn't going to stand in your way to make music, even if all you could play was some card tricks. I just wanted to make sure that we educated our audience as we entertained them, by reading from my book.

ORIENTO

My thoughts exactly. See this saw? Not only can I cut things, and build things with it, but you know that I can take this here yardstick and play this here saw to sound like a space ship.

(Strokes the steel yardstick across the back of the saw)

FRANKLIN

(Huffily) Well, you may be able to thwang that thing, but if you want to hear real music, you just need to listen to my sax. Talk about soothing, when I give a concert with this instrument, everyone listens. Wait until we find that mandocello, that'll really be hot!

(Plays a short riff on the sax)

JASON

(Matter-of-factly) Speaking of hot, now that the sun's been up for a while, it really is getting warm out here. I hope the wind holds up, otherwise, you're right, without a motor we may be searching for that new instrument for quite some time, more than we've already been on this ride.

JUANITA

(Gloomily) And we've already been doing this for longer than I've been a schoolteacher. If I wasn't musically mission-driven, I would be starting to get tired of this.

ORIENTO

(Shockingly) Starting to get tired? If I have to keep playing this saw, I'm going to fall asleep. I need to pull on something, like a mandocello.

DONATARI

Hey, at least you can make some music. I can just make noise by shuffling these cards. I need an instrument too, like a mandocello.

(Shuffles the deck noisily one time)

FRANKLIN

How about me? Even though I can really swing with my sax, pushing on these valves makes my fingers tired. I want a change too, I want strings. I want a mandocello.

(Fingers a short riff on the sax, but does not play it)

JASON

And how about me? I can swing on this tiller, but all I ever hear is water swishing behind me. I need to pluck something, like a mandocello.

JUANITA

Yeah, well turning the pages of this book doesn't cut it for me as concertmaster either. I want to strum something, like a mandocello, and we all need to eat. Pass some of that asafetida.

(Closes her book with a snap)

About the Author

About the Author

Larry Samuels currently lives on the Eastern Shore of Maryland, and for the past eleven years, with his inspirational wife of thirty-two years, Marguerite, who is a former adjunct professor of English at a major university, as well as previously holding a position as an English tutor and academic counselor at a community college. In addition, she has taught a college preparation course to high school students, scores Advanced Placement (AP) essays, and is a former elementary and middle school teacher. She currently provides one-on-one direct care employment specialties for adults with various developmental disabilities. Larry and Marguerite have one son, Paul, in his early twenties, and a daughter, Rebecca, in her late teens.

Formerly a resident of New York City, Larry spent his youth and adult life moving many times within the city and elsewhere, counting fourteen addresses as of this writing. He was in the Boy Scouts, played handball in schoolyards, played stickball and other games in the streets, and worked at many part-time jobs in his neighborhoods, since the age of thirteen.

Following high school graduation, taking a selection of college courses and filling-in with several part-time jobs, he left school, and worked as a taxicab driver throughout the city before enlisting in the U.S. Navy during Vietnam.

During four years' active service, he achieved the rate of E-5 / Petty Officer 2nd Class, with a rating of Boiler Tender (BT) operating and repairing high-pressure steam plants, on a guided missile destroyer which provided gun-fire support off the coast of Vietnam in the Gulf of Tonkin for ground operations in-country, and then on a destroyer escort along the coast of Africa, in the Middle East, and through the Suez Canal.

Following military service, he continued his college education and also worked for several years in various mechanical technology positions, including three years at the Brooklyn Navy Yard repairing ships boilers. He also attained his Refrigeration Machine Operators License and ran a stationary plant of vintage 1920s equipment, which included assignment as an elevator service mechanic. Following these positions, he was employed in his career profession as the Facilities & Capital Construction Coordinator for almost thirty years at a large non-profit public library.

While at the library, as a dad, he served as a Cub Scout leader, as an adult Scout leader trainer, as a member of the local Scout District Council and as a Sunday school teacher, along with Marguerite as Program Director, in addition to serving in several other capacities at his church.

Although now retired from the library, he is currently employed, for the past six years, as a substitute teacher for two county public school systems in grades pre-school through high school, for general and special education classes.

He is also involved in his community, volunteering under a formal State-wide program as a youth character development coach, as Secretary of the Board of Directors of a youth sports and academic mentoring program, and as President of the Board of a non-profit organization providing services and advocacy for adults challenged with mental illness and behavioral health recovery.

He serves as a member of a local grass-roots organization, the Social Action Committee for Racial Justice, and as an active committee member with the Kent County chapter of the National Association for the Advancement of Colored People (NAACP).

In addition, he serves as the construction grants manager, and in other capacities, for efforts to preserve and restore a local historic African American church. In conjunction with the Grand Army of the Republic American Legion Post in his town, established by black Civil War veterans, one of only two such posts remaining in the nation, and in coordination with the local historical society, he is Chair of the Legacy Day Vendor Sub-Committee. This annual county-wide event celebrates local African American history and culture.

He is also involved in several leadership roles at his own historic church, including that of Senior Warden of the Vestry, Property Committee Chair, Usher, former Cemetery Warden, as a Youth Shepherd, and participates in the church's Hispanic Mission. He also participates in two Property Management Committees for the Episcopal Diocese of Easton, contributing facilities management and renovation project expertise.

He is a member of a local writer's group that promotes the fundamentals of fiction, non-fiction expression, and the development of advanced projects. He was a contributing author, along with Marguerite, for collections of prose and poetry published by the group and was a contributing editor for the publication of non-fiction works by two members.

He published his first collection of fiction in 2014, *Pay the Price and Other Stories,* relating his experiences during military service, including world travel and human relationships. He also maintains membership in several Veterans organizations.

For these accomplishments and community activities, in January 2017 he was recognized by the Chester Valley Ministers Association of Maryland's Kent County with presentation of their annual Martin Luther King, Jr. Humanitarian Award.

Still working on revising several of his previously written stories, and writing new ones, he is pleased to continue being creative and productive in his writing, to share in family activities, and to participate in community service initiatives.

Book Content History

<u>Introduction:</u>

September 24, 2011 - October 10, 2016 – August 27, 2017 – June 20, 2018 – November 21, 2018 – January 26, 2019

<u>Manuscript:</u>

September 26, 2015 – October 10, 2016 – August 27, 2017 – June 5, 2018 – January 27, 2019